Cabinet
des Fées

Cabinet
des Fées

a fairy tale journal

PRIME BOOKS

Cabinet des Fées
a fairy tale journal
Volume One, No. 1

Copyright © 2006 by **Cabinet des Fées**

Cover by Charles Vess

All interior art by Charles Vess except:

frontispiece: "Snow White" by Hermann Vogel
page 16: R. Andre, illustration for "The Twelve Brothers"
        by the Brothers Grimm
page 38: "The Haunted Wood" by Arthur Rackham
page 66: "Three Witches" by John Bauer

Published by Prime Books
http://www.prime-books.com

For more stories, poetry, art, and information on forthcoming volumes, visit
http://www.cabinet-des-fees.com

CONTENTS

The Commodification of the Fairy Tale
An Introduction to the Alternative

Helen Pilinovsky

IN HIS ESSAY, "The City of Robots" Umberto Eco proposes that "Disneyland makes it clear that within its magic enclosure it is fantasy [and not reality] that is absolutely reproduced." (202) His statement is applicable, not only to the world of the real, but also to the pure world of the imagination; not only to the actuality of Disneyland, but also to their product, the commodified fairy tale. This entity bears only a faint relation to that magical genre of the fantastic originally known as the fairy tale, as can be seen through the examination of the process of distortion that resulted in the creation of the commercialized version most commonly seen today . . . but not always.

This process began in a small way with the French *contes de fées*, but did not truly catch fire until nearly a hundred years later with the works of the Brothers Grimm, after which it continued through the Victorian era, and came to fruition with the advent of the Disney corporation's mass-market, multi-media approach. The combined efforts of these entities, doubtless enhanced by the contributions of other, smaller imitators, combined to present the public with what Baudrillard what might call a simulacrum of the fairy tale; an image of the form and its purpose totally unrelated to what it actually was before the creation of the false image. The simulacrum can be distinguished from the original in two ways; through the didactic message typically discernible beneath the surface of the tale, fitting the goals of the composing society, and through the notion of something for nothing present in the conceptualization of the "happily-ever-after" ending.

Maerchen — a German term which can be loosely translated as tales of wonder — appear in every culture. In France, we have the *contes des fées*, the tales of the fairies. In Russian, we have *skazki*, which can be transliterated simply as tales. Regardless of the term which we use to refer to them, their purpose is still the same; to enchant, to provide potential etiologies, and to communicate through a rich symbolism knowledge which is more difficult to convey through more explicative means. In other times and other cultures, tales of wonder have not been stigmatized as appropriate for one intention or class alone; their magic served a communicative purpose for the community as a whole. Greek myths, Roman legends, Arthurian romances . . . all of these, and myriad others besides, would easily fall into the ghettoized genre of the modern "fairy tale" as it is commonly understood today, yet those tales were shared and utilized by all. Tales of wonder were originally viewed as being appropriate for all ages, and all levels of society; this can be seen in the work of such early fairy tale authors such as Giovan Francesco Straparola, who wrote in 16th century Italy, and Marie-Catherine d'Aulnoy, who wrote in 17th century France, both clearly for mature audiences. As Jack Zipes says in his essay, "Spells of Enchantment," "It has generally been assumed that fairy tales were first created for children and are largely intended for children. Nothing could be further from the truth." (1) It is only after the conception of the genre of children's literature by Rousseau in the late 17th century that fairy tales began to be considered in light of a specific audience. The stories of Charles Perrault were written in the tone of the subversive works of authors such as Marie-Catherine d'Aulnoy and Catherine Bernard; however, unlike those tales, which possessed specific political overtones and acted as mediums for societal criticism, Perrault's tales were marketed as if they were tales for children. This idea was seized upon enthusiastically by the Grimms, and brought into full flower by the Victorians, with their general idealization of the stage of childhood. *Maerchen* became commodities produced for particular purposes and proffered to specific segments of society for purposes both didactic and financial.

In another essay, Zipes astutely commented that, with the bowdlerization of the fairy tale in the Victorian period, it was "almost as though the wings of the fairies had been clipped, for the 'little people' do not represent a threat to the established Victorian norms." (*Victorian Fairy Tales, xxiii*) To expand upon Zipes metaphor for the clipping of the fairies wings, let us for a moment consider seriously what the diminuation of fairies into tiny, adorable creatures meant symbolically. Who presents a more compelling figure . . . Queen Maeve of old Celtic mythology, or Mab the fairy midwife from *Romeo and Juliet*, or, better still, Tinkerbell from *Peter Pan*? Fairy tales have had a long and honorable history of representing the other, as Carole G. Silver notes in her brilliant work *Strange and Secret People: Fairies and Victorian Consciousness*: there, Silver shows how the commodification of the fairy tale served to support the existing power structure by literally diminishing the symbolic other. The smaller the symbol of otherness, the less effective it became as a means of subversive commentary, thus effectively crippling the use of the form for further social commentary, unless it was quite cleverly done. As Zipes puts it, fairy tales can be used "to induce a sense of happy end and ideological consent and to mute [the]

9

subversive potential for the benefit of those social groups controlling power in the public sphere." ("Spells of Enchantment," 27-28) The didacticism of the Victorian period dictated to the goals of a common good rather than individual interest, sublimating the fantastic, the mythic, and the magical as being things unfit for and inapplicable to society as a whole. Those fairy-stories that did remain were rewritten, tailored to suit the perceived needs of the only class of people who they were still seen to suit — children. They were used for the purposes of acculturation and indoctrination, much as they still are today.

In an essay written over a hundred years ago, concerning variants of fairy tales which dealt with fairly serious issues — Aarne-Thompson type 510B, for example, which deals with the topic of incest — Andrew Lang wrote "On the first view [of these stories] I was horrified at the sight of these skeletons within the tale. It was as if one had a glimpse into the place where Hop o'my Thumb's Giant kept the bones of his little victims. Dry bones of child-like and charming tales are these, a place of many skulls." (Cox, *vii*) The sentiment that mankind has progressed past needing these tales, and that they could better be rewritten to suit modern purposes of didacticism and gain could easily — paraphrased less articulately, perhaps — be placed in the mouth of any Victorian editor, or, to bring matters closer to home, in the mouth of any major shareholder of the Disney corporation, that bastion of virtue that has given us a Little Mermaid with a happy ending in favor of the original spiritual parable (the "happy ending" is far more likely to draw crowds). Regarding the question of whether that is a desirable fact, Jack Zipes asks,

Are fairy tales in America mere commodities that compensate for the technological evolution that has narrowed the range of possibilities for developing the imagination and humane relationships in reality? . . . [The] postmodern fairy tale [reflects] . . . the self-reflective search for a fantastical form that will recuperate the utopian function of the traditional fairy tale in a manner that is commensurate with the major social changes in the postindustrial world. (Zipes, "The Contemporary American Fairy Tale" 139)

These words reflect the ambivalence of the modern world concerning the role of fantasy in the present. Spoken more than a century after the qualms of Victorian critics who saw such stories as being quaint, outmoded, and fit only for children, with these words we examine the other side of the coin — that perhaps the modern world has grown too harsh, too cynical, and too fast-paced to accept the possibilities of deliverance from our troubles by any agency at all, be it through brute power, through carefully applied knowledge, or through their metaphorical representation of magic. The blame has been shifted from the tales to the tellers, upon the actual society as a whole, for growing materialistic, rancorous, and self-involved, for producing tales that draw upon older creations and features of the fairy tale form without attempting to relate them to the issues of modern life, a point which segues nicely into the fact that our current ineffectual commodified fairy tales are not, in fact, fairy tales at all; they are fakelore rather than folklore (to use the words of Alan Dundes), mutton disguised as lamb, in short false images; they are simulacra.

Plato's conception of the simulacrum referred to "the identical image for which no original has ever existed." (Jameson, 74). Baudrillard, in his explanation of that concept, states that "To simulate is to feign to have what one hasn't" (Baudrillard, 1733) That definition is a perfect parallel for the position of the commodified fairy tale in today's society. The purveyors of such tales — Disney and co. — do not have "true" fairy tales; they only have their own distorted versions, only distantly related to any folklore or literature, which they present as the ultimate reality of the genre. Baudrillard also describes them as being "sites of the disappearance of meaning and representation" (Ibid.), which, again, is precisely what Disney and its imitators do to the tales that they bastardize, rather than bothering to craft original material. Not a single Disney rendition of a tale is true to the original that inspired it. Instead, the commodified fairytale holds true to a series of functions (to use a Proppian analysis) which bear little relation to the actual functions of a fairy tale. The characteristics of a simulated fairy tale can be broadly sketched as follows; there are, of course, more functions in existence, waiting to be discovered, but these two markers will do for the nonce. They consist of didactic messages typically clearly discernible beneath the surface of the tale, fitting the goals of the composing society, and through the notion of something for nothing present in the conceptualization of the "happily-ever-after" ending.

The simulated quality of the didacticism of the commodified tale does not stem from the fact that there *is* a message, but rather, from the source and nature of that message. Fairy tales have always served an etiological function; for example, Little Red Riding Hood is typically interpreted to have taught caution and obedience. However, Disney's tales are commonly acknowledged to consistently reinforce the patriarchal hegemony, and the commercial nature of the capitalist system. Presently, the term "fairy tale" now brings to mind associations of unrealistic situations in which everything, however improbably, goes right, where even the tiniest details bear a patina of scrupulous perfection. This is a condition which can only be attained completely through magic, as reality is somewhat less obliging, resulting in the ubiquitous "happily-ever-after." That quality of perfection, however, is not representative of the fairy tale genre as a whole, but rather is a marker of the commodification of the fairy tale; simplifying the genre makes it far more saleable, far more "appropriate" for the target audience.

That phrase, the "target audience", lies at the heart of the issue of commodification: are fairy tales truly fit only for dissemination for children? If not — a given which readers of this journal will probably already hold true, thus negating the necessity of preaching to the choir — what is the alternative? The reversal of commodification is nigh on impossible, failing a full-fledged flight to anarchy; however, broadening the concept of the commodifiable quantity, and thus, expanding its "target audience" is a strategy wholly within our purview. *Cabinet des Fées* would argue that the fairy tale is a form which is as viable today as it was in the past; as much of interest to adults as to children, and, specifically, to readers of all ages who would venture more fully into the intricacies of the stories for their own sakes, to ask why Bluebeard's wife would willingly accept his foibles, how the story differs when it's told from the perspective of the "evil" stepmother, or whether the tale is intrinsically changed by its migration from a given locale or period to another.

Cabinet des Fées takes its name from the 17th century *contes des fées*, the tales of the fairies. In its pages, you will find explorations of their histories set both in fiction, and in fact. This issue brings you a plethora of alternative perspectives. First, we have an exploration of one of the Child Ballad's, "The Gardener", from Catherynne Valente — a regular feature! Sonya Taaffe explores a Pied Piper-like theme in her short piece, "The Fool's Doorway",and Mike Allen carries us to a Dr. Moreau themed fairy tale from the Grimms with "The Music of Bremen Farm". Donna

Quattrone's "All For a Rose" finds us visiting the Beast's castle with a singularly clear-eyed Beauty, and JoSelle Vanderhooft — an author familiar to those of you who enjoyed our first on-line issue — returns with a sorrowfully flavored explication on the birth of a nixie. Lila Garrote presents a bleakly beautiful inversion of "Bluebeard" in her story "Un Conte de Fee", told from a wife's perspective: Virginia Mohlere explores the next stage of the cycle with "All My Mommies", spoken in the voice of Bluebeard's daughter. Finally, a trio of writer explore some lesser-known tales: K. Eason brings us a version of "Little Red Riding Hood" which has more in common with Delarue's version than with Perrault's, though it's still yet darker; Maria Beliaeva ventures into the territory of the Russian folktale with "Owls", a tale which speaks of wolves and *wolves* in its examination of post-Soviet politics; and finally, Maire NicAodh presents us with a story that's half "Corpse Bride" and half dryad's revenge, but all and entirely fascinating. In our academic section, Nick Freedman brings us an examination of one of science fictions great's views on the fee with "H.G. Wells in Fairyland" . . . proof positive that enchantment can lurk where you least expect it. We hope that you enjoy our first issue, and join us in anticipating the other alternatives to commodification!

Bibliography

Bendix, Regina. *In Search of Authenticity*, The University of Wisconsin Press, 1997.

Brooke-Rose, Christine. *A Rhetoric of the Unreal*, Cambridge University Press, 1981.

Cashdan, Sheldon. *The Witch Must Die: How Fairy Tales Shape Our Lives*, Basic Books, 1999.

Dochwerty, Thomas, ed. *Postmodernism: A Reader*, Columbia University Press, 1993.

Leitch, Vincent B., ed. *The Norton Anthology of Theory and Criticism*, W.W. Norton & Co., 2001.

Metzger, Michael M., and Mommsen, Katherine, ed. *Fairy Tales as Ways of Knowing: Essays on Marchen in Psychology, Society, and Literature*, Peter Lang, 1981.

Tatar, Marina. *The Classic Fairy Tales*, W.W. Norton and Company, 1999.

Tatar, Maria. *Off With Their Heads! Fairy Tales and the Culture of Childhood, Princeton University Press*, 1992.

Warner, Marina. *From The Beast to the Blonde*, The Noonday Press, 1994.

Yolen, Jane. *Touch Magic: Fantasy, Faerie, and Folklore in the Literature of Childhood*, Philomel Books, 1981.

Zipes, Jack. *The Great Fairy Tale Tradition*, W.W. Norton and Company, 2001.

Zipes, Jack. *Happily Ever After: Fairy Tales, Children, and the Culture Industry*, Routledge, 1997.

Zipes, Jack. *The Oxford Companion to Fairy Tales*, Oxford University Press, 2000.

Child's Play: #219, *The Gardener*

Catherynne M. Valente

CHILD BALLAD #219, *THE GARDENER*, is at first glance a simple exchange: a young man asks a girl for her hand, and she refuses him. Bertrand Bronson shelves it as "too little of a ballad, generating virtually no story." It is brief, but vivid, consisting of a series of striking natural images: the boy plies his suit with a startling litany of flowers and plants with which he will festoon his love like jewels, promising to cover her in blossoms quite literally from the crown of her head to the tips of her toes.

Her answer is unsettling to say the least. Instead of a simple "no, thank you kindly" she offers him equal measure, of a sort: "Since you've provided a weed for me/ Among the summer flowers/ Then I'll provide another for you/ Among the winter showers." She then offers him a deathly suit of snow, with a crown of freezing wind and a tunic of rain.

While this might be seen as nothing more than an ornate insult on the level of "drop dead," the preponderance and intensity of the imagery—and in a ballad so short, imagery is essentially all there is—indicates the presence of a deeper dialogue at play: that of the eternal elements, circling each other and never touching.

Our two speakers can easily be seen as summer and winter: the earnest, bright-eyed gardener with all his earthy, humble wealth is a clear corollary to the Green Man, while the haughty maid with her suit of snow is redolent of the Snow Queen. They are the Lion and the Unicorn, fighting for the crown, the fertile and the barren, the growing and the sleeping earth. He tries to entice her into his garden, to melt and revel in the sunshine—but of course, she cannot assent, for she is winter incarnate, and the summer is not her kingdom. She offers equal measure: he can join her in December and January, and wear her snow and ice, but he can no more accept those clothes than she can accept his, and they part ways for the season, the status quo maintained. Winter retains her primacy for a few more months, until she can do nothing but yield to the camovine and the keil-blades, and wait for her turn to come again.

The Gardener and the Grave-Keeper

He stood in her doorway like a planted bramble;
    she stood aside,
    and drew away —
but his voice grazed her cheek sun-sallow,
and his whisper
pulled at her gauzy sleeve:

"Under your white wrist I open my jaw
under your cold chin I split my teeth
under you, O colorless , O maid,
I hinge and splay my tongue —
and there is a rose there,
    a red rose, aye, and fair.

You could pluck this thing from me,
    aye, this red, red thing,
and I would be your own brown-bellied boy;
I would sew you up a dress of lilies,

18

a thread of soft stems
(dandelion and daisy, by measure mine)
glinting green in the seam
        for nothing which is not root-pure
        should brush the landscape of your skin.

And I would draw a coat of camellia
over your shoulders, patched with ivy and vine.
I would pull gloves of marigold over your hands,
and I would cinch your waist with a skirt of salad-greens,
sleek your calves with wide, grassy stalks.
And I would cap your hair — O lightless hair! — with gilly-
    flower,
pin primrose to your breast as pearl.

You could pluck this thing from me,
        aye, this red, red thing,
let it stain your pristine fingers —
for I would plant this thing in you,
and erase your flesh with flowers,
vanish you in flora until your own sweet mouth
floods itself with petals,
petals red and fair.

I would cover you in boughs
(if you would not say me nay)
until your belly lay beneath me
framed in sap and green —
then — O then! — I would crack your flesh door-open,
cross you like a threshold,
to find beneath your reedy navel
the hidden sun, gold and pale,
a burning cuff around your spine.

And on this disc, this red, red disc,
I would place my rose,
tongue to bone, tongue to bone.

Say you'll take my rose from me,
say you'll let the sun
dribble out between your hipbones —
I will crown you high in summer sweet,
and feed you from my own bright lips
like the blue-beaked hoopoe
succors her young."

But the white-cheeked maid drew back from him,
and her breath was chill on his chin:

"I will not take that thing from you,
            nay, not that red, red thing —
it would burn me so.

You would melt me all away
and be my sop-soaked boy,
all drenched in my ruin,
all silver with my ruin —
why would you hold such a thing out to me,
bloody and scalding, bloody and bright?

I will not take it, I will not take it —

but you could take this cold from me,
            aye, this pale, pale thing,
and be my own brack-barren boy.

And I could sew you up a smock of snow,
a crown of broken branches;

I could sleek your calves in ice and stone,
I could cap your hair — O downy hair! — in whipping wind,
clap rain to your breast as iron.

I could cover you in sleet
(if you would not say me nay)
until your broad back lay beneath me
framed in yew and howl —
then — O then! — I would crack your skin grave-open
climb you like a stair
and find beneath your hail-strewn bones
the hidden moon, half in shadow,
a breathing ring around your spine.

And on this sickle, this pale, pale scythe,
I would place my freezing kiss,
tongue to bone, tongue to bone."

She stood in her doorway like a twisted ice-slough;
                he stood aside,
                and bolted away
though her voice grazed his cheek moon-fallow,
and her whisper
snagged his coarse-sewn sleeve.

The Fool's Doorway

Sonya Taaffe

HE WELCOMED YOU IN, stumbled with a flourish over the doorstep as he caught open the door that swung inward to a faint click and chime of bells, nailed in loops of ribbon over the painted wood. Images swam out at you, little more than time-rubbed washes of color: a woman half hidden in a furl of black, the moon or a blooming rose white in her hair; a man whose hands fountained birds, the eroded outlines of wings; a serpent pinned beneath a hay fork's tines; a tree burning with fruit shaped like comets or tears. Hands flat on the cool panels, forehead bent to the smell of years soaked into the grain like dye, you almost forgot to step forward. A cough, a castanet-clatter of snapped fingers reminded you; a moth-dust of gilt printed your fingertips when you took them away. You stepped through, into the dark.

At first you had taken him for a street musician, then something made you look twice. For a moment you were sure of nothing: the gender of the quick, neat-boned face beneath the loose hair, the paint smudged red and black; the color of the eyes, glass kaleidoscopes drawing color from whatever they were turned on; the thought moving like an unnamed color in them. The sound of his tambourine pulled you closer, inward, until you forgot what you had been doing before you heard the way his fingers drummed, until you set your feet in his footprints down the street that turned in a way you did not remember, exact and unerring as though his loping, graceless, dancing gait had taken you into a place that existed only for the walking. How young he was, you realized when he turned back to wave you on, laughing, tripping slightly over the curb, his face as unfinished as the rest of him; then he stepped down into the street again, and you saw that he walked like an old man.

Downtown brick and concrete had melted away, and you walked among the houses of an alien era, iron railings and columned porches, slate shingles and weathervanes spinning in winds that could not have blown from the same direction twice; curtains lidded the windows, or the glass was flawed and refracted your gaze back at you, and you recognized the flowers growing in front gardens only from books of places you had never been. His tambourine chivvied your feet on when you stopped to stare. On the porch of a house that leaned so far into the grey sky, you wondered what would happen if the sky simply moved aside one half step — would everything come falling down? — he held the door open for you, clumsy and courteous, and you could not meet his inconstant eyes. "You have nothing to fear," he said, all he said, "but nothing itself."

Then the sound of bells glittered in the dark, and he was laughing; you had chosen, and you were elsewhere.

Sonya Taaffe has a confirmed addiction to folklore, mythology, and dead languages. A respectable amount of her work has recently been collected in Singing Innocence and Experience *and* Postcards from the Province of Hyphens *(Prime Books). She is currently pursuing a Ph.D. in Classics at Yale University and has trouble talking about herself in the third person.)*

Une Conte de Fée

Lila Garrott

WE WERE MARRIED AT MIDNIGHT, which was as I had
wished it, although not outside. He insisted on a church and
I acquiesced when I saw the great stained glass window that
hung behind the altar, showing an angel with bronze-gold
wings outspread speaking to some graybeard of a prophet.
The candles that surrounded us everywhere winked like the
stars I had wanted. The blue dusk underneath the Gothic
columns, arches, and buttresses could almost have been that
of a forest. He had ordered more flowers than I had seen
before in one place in my life, and scattered them throughout
the nave so that they displayed themselves along the walls, in
the fonts, at the frames of the windows, twined on the backs
of the pews, and in the hair of the company assembled. All
of the flowers were white and they glowed in the half-light
till I could have seen them as candles themselves. My dress
was a radiance around me and as we walked back from the
altar toward the church door he took my hand and whispered to me "You are the moon." The throngs of our friends
and my relatives cheered us into our carriage. The beauty of
the occasion made up in the eyes of our spectators for the
absurdity of the hour, and it had already been lent some
respectability by the waning custom of the midnight Mass;
but nothing could forestall the whispers about the hastiness
of the wedding. I had taken his hand for the first time three
months earlier, and bowed over it as he bowed to me, in a
room full of candles as well, and had watched him smile like
an alabaster statue awaked to sudden mirth. We had danced

that evening and every evening since, for he courted with the ardor with which he made his money and from the moment I first saw him I knew what was to happen.

For there was no denying my husband. He moved with lazy grace through the world and the world gave way before him as it would have to a jungle-cat. What he wanted he would have and it was a matter of auspicious circumstance that his desires and mine should happen to coincide so neatly, to dovetail into a perfect ring like the white gold that finally sealed our marriage on my finger. It bore no carving or inscription but upheld a ruby that had been in his family since the Dark Ages. It flashed in the intermittent lamplight through the windows as the carriage bore us homewards from our wedding, but it could not have been as bright as my pride. We reached the house; he helped me from the carriage; he unlocked the front door with the great ring of keys that he wore at his belt; I went to take off my lace and satin finery; and finally, when all was ready, I went and stood before his carved-mahogany door, and the lamp in my hand made my ring flash the brighter as I pounded. That door might have been fixed since the beginning of time for all it moved or for all the sound I heard within. I searched the rest of the house for my husband and came upon nothing but wing after wing of polished wood and polished marble and windows whose tinted glass let in the actual moon in a thousand different shades of subtle light. The doors stood closed and locked and the rooms unbreachable, every one of them. I surmised he must carry the keys around with him continually in that large, archaic ring. I found I could not even open a window to let in a breath of air for it was a house of keyholes, bars, and silences and in all that palatial emptiness nothing moved except myself. I went to the room I had left my dress in, finally, and heard the lock click behind me as I lay there in puzzled awareness throughout my first night as a wife.

I had thought that it might take some time for him to become close to me and accustomed to my presence, but I had not expected the elemental shyness that greeted me in the days and weeks that followed. He treated me with punctilious courtesy and when my friends from the galleries and studios came to see me of an evening he left with perfect grace and with rapidity. I knew that death had wrought its havoc on his ordered life before this and that he might not bear my confidence in our bargain, and so I tried to reassure him with my presence and assure him of my devotion in every way left open to me. I very rarely went out, not even to see those promising young artists who had been my protégées before my marriage. I was patient, which is a thing against my nature, and I smiled when I saw him even if it was in passing. I brought him tea and toast in the mornings in the soft blue music room where he sat at a small octagonal table with his newspaper, and then I played the piano (badly) for him before he left the house to see about his business. I met him in the library when he came home in the evenings, where the curtains blew out into the garden and the fireflies twinkled through the fluttering lace. We spoke of utter nothing while the evenings darkened and the light glinted on the wall of locked, glass-fronted bookcases. I never asked that anything be opened for me. I was calm and cheery and predictable and all the while my husband, the white lion, drew further and further away into himself until his resemblance to a statue was more marked than ever and I deluded myself his mouth might crack if he expressed any emotion with it. He smiled like a slender, glacial Buddha, spoke when he was spoken to, and continued to bolt his door in the evenings.

I was left to myself for the majority of the time and since I had determined to discontinue the round of social gatherings I had inhabited previously it was inevitable that my mind should turn itself backwards in remembrance and reflection. Each stroke of each one of my paintings revisited me in its carmine or olive or violet, and as well the faces of the buyers, inextricably linked in my mind to my art as a setting is to a jewel. I saw again the reviews of my shows and my competitive entries, and the glowing words and offers from the representatives of museums. I smelled turpentine in my sleep, and woke to the memory of the sureties and subtleties that had dwelt in my hands. I lived it all again, moment by moment, while the ashes of my final painting brooded in a small leather box on my nightstand, while my husband grew ever more distant, and while I became more and more determinedly pleasant. I ceased to entertain in the evenings, but the shadows would not leave my conscious-ness. It was the newspaper that undid me at the last. I picked it up one morning in the music room just after he had left the house, in the hope of finding an occupation for the long time until lunch. One of my young friends had finally had a solo exhibition, and the reviewer was both astounded and delighted. This friend credited me as her great source and inspiration, and mourned the cessation of my achievements, also claiming to the reviewer that my discourses on theology had revolutionized her intellect. The reproduced painting that accompanied the article was a chiaroscuro of the archangel Michael falling from Heaven, great wings shred-ding and falling to bits in an unseen wind that forced him downwards. At the sight of this magnificence I dropped the paper and burst into tears. I sobbed for nearly an hour and could not regain any control whatsoever.

I didn't hear the door open, didn't hear him come in from his work early; I had no knowledge of his presence until he was wiping the tears from my face with his handker-chief. His arms were around me and his voice was soothing and slow. I cradled my face against the softness of his coat until I ceased crying, and was then guided to my feet, his hands still gentle and insistent on my shoulders. He put an arm around me and walked me to the door, and then through the hallways of the great mansion I had almost stopped exploring for lack of any entrance to more than perhaps seven of its chambers. I glanced up at him, sideways, as we strolled, and saw through my pain that the look on his face was that of one who sees come with weary resignation a thing that he has long expected. My heart leaped within me, and a strange exultation ran me through in spite of my still-shuddering shoulders. Now, maybe. Now.

He led me, however, to a room I had not seen before, whose door was carved of rowanwood in peculiar, soft red patterns, and unlocked it with a key from his inevitable key-ring. The walls of the room on three sides were of glass, and the sunlight streamed in. Set at precisely the correct angle to catch the morning brilliance were a very fine easel and stool, an artist's palette, and a pile of ready-stretched canvas of the finest quality. The paint was lined in even rows in a set of shelves, and I could see that every possible gradation of color was present. There were brushes, assembled by size; charcoal; ink; paper. I had never owned such a well and painstakingly equipped studio, or hoped to.

"I thought you might be in some need of this," he said. The enormity of the gesture swept over me and I clung to his neck and burst into tears again in a manner I would ordinarily have found to be terribly sentimental.

"I can't," I said, "thank you," when I had mastered my voice. "I can't paint any more." He looked startled, and suddenly wary.

"Is that just because we've gotten married--" he ventured, and I cut him off.

"Oh, of course not! It's far simpler. I can't paint any-more." There was silence for a moment. "Have you ever killed anything?" He grew warier still.

"You can't kill a talent," he said firmly, "and you certainly cannot kill genius."

"Which mine was."

"Which yours was."

"No," I said wearily, "you can't. And I haven't. That was not what I meant to say at all. Thank you again, sir. It was terribly sweet of you. I regret informing you that your kindness has been wasted, but I shall never paint again. Can never. I am sorry." The caution eased in his face and he pulled me closer to him until we stood fully embraced for the first time in our marriage.

"I am sorry too." We stood like that for quite some while, as the sun poured in through the windows, and I looked at the fine lines of his face with some enjoyment. When he spoke, his voice was unexpected, calm in the silence. "Would you like a child?" It took me a moment to decipher what he'd said, and he continued. "It would occupy your time." I was startled into shaky laughter by that.

"Oh no," I told him carefully, as my laughter was becoming hysterical because of the emotional tempests I had experienced over the course of the day. "But thank you . . . anyway . . . for asking . . ." And with that I was truly laughing fully, for the first time in at least a year, so that my husband smiled to see it, a real smile. I was taken unawares yet again when he bent over to kiss me. I am not generally easily surprised. It was in itself a surprise to me how many times that day I had been caught by the unexpected. His kiss, however, was the greatest shock thus far. We lost ourselves in it, and he pulled away from me only to prowl around me, running hands over my shoulders, my arms, my back, and then returning to my face so I could fall into his mouth again. He backed me up against the fresh canvas that stood on my useless new easel, and laid his lips above my heart. His pocket-watch chimed, and I cursed it inwardly, for at the sound he stood again, brushing at his knees, and stated with his deep regrets that he was late for an appointment which could not possibly be missed.

It was some time before I pulled myself to my feet from where I half reclined against the easel. A fierceness had awakened in me that I had not felt since I set the fire that claimed my last and greatest painting. I felt some desire to go and comb through the ashes again, to remind myself of my talent, and of who I was, and why I had left the world of art. It took extreme self-control to prevent myself from doing this. I would not revel in my fall from glory. Gathering my thoughts together finally from their scatter, I walked towards the door, and then stopped and turned at a splash of color that caught the corner of my vision. Upon the canvas, where it must have smeared itself from the soft white dress I was wearing, was a perfect cross in alizarin crimson, as dark and as red as the ruby on my finger. It was almost the shade of dried blood. I peered down my back as best I could, seeing that he must have painted this when he had walked around me, and painted it, indeed, with his own fingers. The paint extended from the nape of my neck to the base of my spine, and across the widest span of my shoulders. It had not been properly mixed and lumps of pigment were still damply trickling down from the crossbar. I left the room to go and change my gown, grinning all the while in the grip of that delighted fierceness. I did not wash the gown, but draped it over the wardrobe door where the cross would catch the light. It very nearly completely covered the mirror. The rest of the day was a blur to me, but that cross burned through the haze like a beacon whenever I caught sight of it. I would never wear that gown again; it was too beautiful to move.

* * *

He did not bolt his door that night, as I had known he wouldn't. The look on his face when I came in was almost invitation, and that was enough. It was a dark room, in the same mahogany as his door, and decorated with prints and carvings of lions hunting. Pictures of other kinds of animals ran riot on the molding and on the canopy of his bed, done in oils and in embroidery by a skilled and delicate hand. There were whole menageries in inches of that chamber, although among all the fur and scale and hide and hoof there could be seen no winged or feathered thing. He was in bed, and his dressing-gown was wine-colored velvet.

"Do you believe in angels?" I inquired as I moved to sit next to him at the head of the huge four-poster. "You look a good deal like one. Shouldn't you be telling me not to be afraid?"

"I've been married before, three times," he said. "You certainly have the right to be afraid, if you should want to."

"I'm not an innocent," I said lightly, before I bent to kiss him. He drew me down beside him, and a noise arose in the room as if all the animals that lurked in wood and moiré were giving tongue at once, but I was far too occupied to seek the source of it. I was attempting to get him to remove the dressing-gown while he made love to me, a battle which I lost decisively and permanently. I could have any of him that did not require him to disrobe himself—but what we did was sufficient to me, and I thought more might be forthcoming in the future. I supposed that one could not, after all, shed shyness such as his in just one evening, even for love and in my perfect safety. Afterward, I slept in his arms against warmth and the tangles of velvet. I dreamed of mighty wings, and of oils, of brushes, of chiaroscuro and sorrow.

* * *

I awoke in continued darkness, for the windows of his room were barred by heavy draperies of that same wine-colored velvet, and he had not opened them when he got himself up and left. His dressing table was disarranged and I could see that he had shaved, had combed his hair and drunk water, while I continued fast asleep. The room was warm and I lay for a while in the peculiar darkness that only comes to closed-off rooms in the heat of summer noon. After a while something white caught my eye, which was not my night-gown, for that garment was under my pillow and this was on the seat of a heavy wood chair near the door. I rose, and stretched languorously, unable to hurry in the sultry dark, before I picked the envelope he had left me off the cushion. It had on the front of it the two words "My Own".

The letter praised my beauty, my wittiness, and my sensuality before continuing to state that deeply as he loved me and much as he had been in bliss he must needs hasten away for out-of-town business that would sadly take him at least a fortnight to complete. He had taken the liberty of leaving before I awakened as he could not bear to commit the crime of waking someone as vital as myself from a necessary slumber. He hoped I would forgive him this and be placated by the delight of being the chatelaine of his estate during his absence, he having left me (enclosed) the keys to the rooms, doors, windows, chests, and bookcases of the establishment. He remained, as ever, my dearly loving husband. I had to admire the manner in which he combined his habitual excessive formality with the words of a great and fervent passion. I could see in my mind just how he would have pronounced to me the words he had written, and the thought made me smile. The key-ring rattled in the envelope as I held it through the paper, and I drew it out and placed it around my finger beside the great ruby. In the half-light the keys appeared the same gold as that ring, twin symbols of the same contract. My time had come, and I was happy in my love for him, which was at last bringing itself to fruition.

It remained for me in the hours that followed to go carefully through the house, examining my newfound treasure. There were doors of olivewood and doors of iron, doors of ebony and doors of teak, doors carved, doors painted, doors filigreed, and one small door that was etched and enameled. There were doors with huge padlocks and doors with tiny locks suitable for dollhouses, doors with many locks and doors with one. They were every one of them locked. I knew each one would open to the keyring on my finger, but I touched nothing in the mansion as I passed through it. I did not open any doors, until I at last discovered one that proved to be close to my own bedroom: a flat, featureless expanse of some black metal whose rusted doorknob of pig iron bore upon it no padlock whatsoever. Here might anyone have entered. I opened it slowly, for it was heavy, and opened outwards, which necessitated my walking entirely around it once it had shifted enough to leave a passage for my slender body.

The room within was stark in its design and hermetic in its simplicity. The walls were painted an exact bone white. There were no windows. I found nothing in it that I had not expected. I knelt on the floor, in an attitude resembling prayer, facing away from the door, and waited to hear the slight creak which would foretell the door being opened by my lord's much greater bulk. He came. His shadow fell over me from the doorway. I stood, my head bent so that he would not see my smile. I turned. I raised my head.

He stood naked above me, and his revealed body was as sexless as an unmarked sheet of paper. His wings were fire-burnished, as red as the ruby on my finger, as gold as the keys of the paths of his castle. His eyes caught the light of them, dancing, golden, crimson, a furious flicker that had burned forever and would burn when I was dust, and dust of dust. Feathers twined in his hair, and the restless pinions danced with life, scorching the doorframe as they brushed it but leaving no mark on his ivory skin. There were eyes in those feathers, like those of a peacock, except that these eyes burned with the sudden radiance of those set in his head. Fluid ran from these eyes in his feathers, a dark and sticky-looking fluid that collected in drips and dollops on the hissing hardwood flooring. I could not tell whether they wept or bled, or indeed if there would be any difference. O my lover. O my lover. I backed away from him, since he would expect it, and stood against the wall on which were carved the names of his three previous wives. Not a trophy-taker, this one, not a despoiler; he was too noble for that and I knew that my bones would go to ground with the same painstaking care and dignity that he lavished on everything he'd ever loved. The heat radiating from him was great enough to make me think I might catch fire and I shuddered at the sweetened irony of that. He came to me, moving with a pure and simple grace I sighed to watch. He placed his hands around my neck, and as the blackness began to come over my vision I rejoiced for the first time in over a year, I would have cried out if I could have with the fullness of my joy in consummation. At last. Finally. Now. And soon all paid, my best beloved, my angel with the heart of fire. Soon my own heart would be whole again, and my place found, another name on this white and bitter wall, to watch his wives come and go over decades and to paint in my darkness of death the memory of his light, his glory. The world was already beginning to fade.

But he let go of me, and was a man again as much as he could be. He was a man, falling at my feet, begging my forgiveness, crying for my art. No matter that I said I would not paint again; he would not let his artist leave this world in such a manner. For after all, didn't he love me? Had I not had more of him than anyone? His wings subsided, and faded into thin air, with a crumpling and a tattering. They left after them an ashiness, as of a great bonfire going out. There were twin scars down his shoulderblades, along his spine, and his eyes were merely yellow again, like the eyes of a tame lion. The ruby on my finger evanesced into the brightening air, and the keys fell onto the floor with a clatter. His face was full of agony, but he strove not to show it, smiling up at me as a man who has seen Paradise. It was Paradise I knew he left behind him; I knew he felt great love for me that he would fall at my feet this way, and keep falling, invisibly, in that merciless wind my friend had painted. He made no motion but I knew that he descended vasty fathoms for me. At length he reached the bottom. I shuddered there, for his sake, but the choice was his, and always had been. There was nothing I could have done for him, even if I had wanted to.

I kicked him in the ribs. I clawed him with my nails until the blood ran down that snow-white body. I spat on him and pinched him and kicked him over and over, before I left him there in his pain and went to my room and returned with the little leather box full of ashes. I sprinkled them over him, gently, like falling snow and soot, and only at that did he cry out in pain, for they know their own kind and they know their own death; all that host know it, all of who he had been. I rubbed that ash into the scars of his wings as I told of my first lover, who also bore fire on his back, a rainbow fire, and who carried a trumpet that when winded would kill all things that were alive or dead already. I had loved my lover but my first love had been art and of all the things to paint that I had ever seen nothing was half so beautiful as the murdered, writhing body of that seraph. I had burned my talent out in a flash of incendiary lightning and lust, and the masterpiece that had resulted I had also destroyed, when I came to my senses, before the eyes of innocents could see it. And he who should have been my punishment learned there in the ashes of what it means to betray utterly one's nature, as I had learned before him, as may someday all of the legions of Michael.

I paint again now, in that sweet little studio. These new works are not for any public exhibition, being as they are tonal studies in red, mostly. He is sick in my arms and he shivers in the hot summer nights. I have never seen him so beautiful as when he is bleeding for me. I do not know how long he may survive, in this way, here, with me, my husband. I love him more than I have words to say to him, and so I will not ask him if he might still live forever. I think that I would like him to.

Lila Garrott lives in Cambridge, MA with her wife, six housemates and two cats. She has previously sold short fiction to Not One of Us *and poetry to* Jabberwocky, *as well as criticism to the* Internet Review of Science Fiction.

The Music of Bremen Farm

Mike Allen

BUT FOR A FLAT TIRE, no one would have known that Old Hag Bremen was dead.

Her forebears, like other settlers from Germany, staked out plots in the shadows of the sloping Blue Ridge Mountains even before the white colonies declared themselves a nation. Throughout the rolling hills where houses regard each other across wide vales and narrow roads still ford streams with wooden bridges held together by iron spikes, the Anglicized names speak from rusting mailboxes: Anselm. Flohr. Krone. Newman. Schrader.

Yet even in this place of isolation, with corn blanketing the hills for miles before giving way to ancient mountain slopes and defiant oak, the Bremens stayed a world apart. They sent no sons to fight in the War of Northern Aggression. They did not come to the whitewashed A-frame churches. They did not grow crops, or ask for work in others' cattle farms or dairies or tobacco fields. Those few who knew the business of the Bremen family left them to it, and spoke of it at most in late night whispers that by morning seemed more like troubled, half-forgotten dreams.

By the time the single-lane dirt ruts finally gave way to asphalt, only one Bremen remained, a sad, solitary heir rattling alone in a rambling home more than 300 years old: still with an outhouse, still with the kitchen standing separate from the building where she made her bed. Only the squirrels and wasps that took shelter in the walls kept her company.

The rotten roof of the family barn, which only ever held what animals the family needed for themselves, had partially collapsed under a heavy snow around the time of the Korean War. She had never tried to have it fixed, and no one had ever offered to do it for her.

No one was even certain of her name, but the children who on dares spied through her windows called her "Old Hag" and that seemed fitting enough.

Folks in the nearest semblance of a town, about five miles away, rarely saw her, and on the few occasions she ventured in to buy simple things like bread or grapefruit juice, she never spoke. The fact is, the cashiers who found this pale, smelly, shriveled woman with grey eyes and long unkempt hair staring at them across the counter were grateful for her silence.

Only the children had any inkling how Old Hag Bremen spent her days, and those inklings came from short, frightened glimpses after dark. They returned whispering of how she shuffled in shadow through what was once one of her ancestor's bedrooms, moving among strange colored flames and glassware filled with bubbling fluid.

Those whispers protected her as well as any fence, until things began to change in the county where she lived. The people there elected a new prosecutor, an aggressive, agitated young man from the North named Edward Jacobs. Echoes of those whispers reached his ears, and he took the scene they described to mean something rather different from what the native folk believed.

The sheriff, a tall, lean, leathery man born and bred in those hills, argued to Jacobs that he should leave well enough alone, that the old lady hurt no one, but at last deferred to the prosecutor's wishes, as the law required, and sent two men in the dead of night to spy. They came back, and talked of a laboratory, and chemicals, and Old Hag Bremen downing the liquids brewed in her beakers. The next night, six more men went, with rifles and a search warrant. They brought the old woman back to the jail, seized her glass equipment and destroyed it.

She spent a month in the city jail to the south, as the county jail had no place to house women. But after that month, she was free, as the state's lab tests found no evidence a crime. Nothing that she had kept in her possession, nothing she had brewed, was against the law.

An innocent passerby, a stout laborer from a neighboring county, discovered her death a mere three months after her return to her family's farm. He'd spent a day sawing down trees on the slopes adjoining her property, and as he drove his pickup down the unpaved logging trail he blew a tire. Discovering his spare was no good, he walked to the sprawling old house he could see through the trees in hopes of using a phone.

The second thing he noticed when he neared the old log house was the smell: the overpowering stench of a body. The third thing he noticed was the flies swarming on the inside of the windows.

He had noticed something else first: a thin strain of music, tinny notes that conformed to no melody but still made him catch his breath and strain to hear, as if someone were singing and he couldn't quite make out the words. But the second and third things made him forget the music, made him run along the long and overgrown path from the house to the nearest paved road, and frantically wave down a logging truck as it groaned around a curve.

The volunteer ambulance workers found the old woman in an indescribable state. Her pale, shriveled hands clutched a music box, an ancient heirloom from the Old Country, so tarnished and corroded that whatever song it held might have been silent for centuries.

* * *

When Jacobs learned of the old woman's death, he felt a twinge of sadness, a fleeting sense of guilt, but no regret, no lasting sorrow. Mostly what moved behind his close-set brown eyes was a sense of relief. He didn't celebrate her death, but her passing, to his mind, made the world a simpler, safer place.

He did experience a different kind of regret, as proving this reviled woman a criminal would certainly have boosted his standing, politically and socially, in this community where he otherwise might always remain an outsider. He believed that if he had a close eye kept on her, that opportunity would have come sure as sunrise. His one meeting with Old Hag Bremen (whose real name, he knew, was Adelia) convinced him of it. A week after her release from jail, she had come to his office to demand compensation for the destruction of her lab.

No one who lived in the county seat, nearly thirty miles from her land, had ever seen her there before. Jacobs' elderly secretary, inherited from the previous top lawman, cut short a scream when she saw the hag sitting in the lobby in a tattered dress grey as ash, her brittle grey locks draped past her waist. Her pale face peered from between the tangles of her hair, grey eyes cold and unblinking as she stared up at the quailing woman and rasped two words: "Edward Jacobs."

Jacobs had seen many unpleasant things, even in his short career, but he grew queasy at the sight of this nightmare woman, terrible and pathetic at once, sitting across the desk from him, utterly out of place amidst the crisp law books on the shelves, degrees and paintings of sailing ships on the walls, the photographs of smiling wife and baby that watched over his fingertips as he drummed them. He had held the leather visitor's chair for her, then had taken his seat and waited for her to speak.

When she did, it was like ice cracking. "You owe me."

Poker-faced, Jacobs replied, "I don't think so."

"You destroyed my dignity," she said. "How can I ever get that back? The least you can do is give me the money to replace the physical things you destroyed."

"I don't think so," Jacobs replied.

She stood, slammed both hands on his desk, and he flinched despite himself. "You ruined any chance I had to restore my family's fortune!"

Jacobs cocked his head, folded his arms and smirked.

"So much of what my ancestors had is gone. What they owned. What they knew. There was still one way I could bring back glory to my family's name, and you took it from me!"

"Lead into gold?" the prosecutor sneered. Old Hag Bremen trembled with rage, but Jacobs interrupted when tried to speak.

"Woman," he said — he couldn't bring himself to call her lady —"I don't know how you did it. How you fooled the lab tests. But I don't believe this story you're spinning, not for a minute. Your house isn't made of gingerbread. If I have my say, you won't have your lab back, and mine is the only say that matters."

She snarled. "You think you understand, but you don't, not one bit."

"I don't need to understand." He stood up, and glared down at her. He wasn't a tall man, but for all his visitor's fearsomeness, he loomed over her by a head. "Get out."

But she wasn't looking at him. Eyes focused somewhere distant, she muttered his name, then repeated it.

"Don't do that," he said.

"I'll call the musicians. They were with my family in the Old Country. They're in the other Old Country now. But there's still a way that they can hear me. It may be the death of me, but they'll come."

"Get out."

"The story they tell about the musicians is all fiction, Mr. Jacobs. The real robbers never left our house alive."

"Get out!"

Jacobs had taken swiftly to wearing a shoulder-holstered pistol beneath his jacket once he'd learned of that particular affectation of Southern prosecutors. He pushed back the flap of the blue suitcoat he wore and put his hand on the pistol's cold grip, making sure the old hag could see it. "Go!"

The hag stared, long enough that he prepared to shout again, his agitation and, yes, fear, building as each second passed. But when he opened his mouth, she turned and left without another word.

Jacobs heard no more from her, until the discovery of her death.

Jacobs sat in the passenger seat and another deputy rode in the back, as the sheriff drove over steepening hills and through switchback turns toward the Bremen farm.

The old hag's body had been removed, and still lay in the city morgue an hour south, unclaimed by any family, as she had none. Now that the house could be endured without wearing a mask, two deputies had gone to inspect the place with gloved hands in search of any evidence of foul play.

Jacobs had ordered the sheriff not to send any more men than those two, not even to secure the scene with yellow tape. "If we do that someone's sure to notice, and then they'll call the press. We don't need any reporters asking about this right now."

Most of the ride unfolded in awkward silence. As he turned onto the final stretch of road before the house, the sheriff looked at Jacobs sidelong. "What if it's a murder, son? You can't sit on that. You can't keep people from finding out."

Jacobs clenched his jaw. "Then we control what they find out. Every word of it."

Besides, murder seemed unlikely. From the description of the condition of the old woman's body, it sounded as if she had been savaged by animals, perhaps wild dogs, or a bear. Bears were such a common problem that one had actually wandered down the main street of the county seat and through the automatic doors into the hospital, where a game warden had to put it out of its beastly misery.

The sheriff barked into his radio as they pulled off the road and parked, asking the men for their locations. No answer came, causing the sheriff to grumble about outdated equipment. It wasn't at all uncommon for firefighters or deputies to respond to calls in the county's far corners and discover their radios no longer worked over long ranges.

The trio hiked toward the house through the woods, but as they came within short range, the sheriff still couldn't raise a response from his men—not even as the log buildings came in view. The sheriff drew his revolver, and the deputy cocked his rifle.

Jacobs drew the pistol from beneath his coat. The sheriff glanced at him sidelong again, his voice shaded with contempt. "You really think you know how to use that?"

"Yes," Jacobs snapped.

"I just don't want you to shoot me by mistake," the sheriff said, with an emphasis on "mistake" that Jacobs didn't like at all. Before he could reply, the sheriff walked to the main part of the house, the building that held the bedrooms, where the old woman's body had lain. He shouted the names of his men, but again, no answer. He gestured to his deputy, who circled around to the back. The sheriff stepped onto the front stoop and tried the door, which opened with a loud wooden groan. Silent as a puma, the sheriff slipped into the darkness within. Jacobs followed, not so silently.

Though the foyer was dark, beams of light sliced through the rooms beyond, piercing through holes in the chinking and gaps between the roof boards. The foyer let out into a sitting room where chairs stood sentry that had once been ornate and grandiose, but were now splintered and mildewed, feather down bleeding out through rips in the stained cushions. The sheriff stood at the door to a different room, sweeping the floor with a small flashlight. He gave a sharp intake of breath, and ducked inside.

Jacobs came in behind, and stopped short. But for the nameplate and badge that glinted in the flashlight beam, there would have been no easy way to recognize the torn body on the floor. Dark stains spattered the walls. No doubt what the stains were.

"Animals," Jacobs said.

The sheriff aimed his flashlight in Jacobs' face. "More men here, and this wouldn't have happened," he said, his voice like red hot iron. "We'll have to get at least a mile away before we're in range to call for back up." When the prosecutor didn't answer, the sheriff pushed past him, shouting the name of the other missing man.

"Sheriff!" called the deputy from outside. "There's blood. It leads up to the barn!"

The ugliest rooster Jacobs had ever seen squawked and scurried from the barn door as the men swung it open. It had no comb and no feathers on its head and neck, and bare pins jutted out here and there like spines from the salt-and-pepper plumage along its flanks. It squawked a second time as the men came inside, and flapped up to land on a beam above the door.

The sheriff asked, "You see any livestock when you came here last?"

The deputy shook his head.

The inside of the barn was in ruins, though apparently, incredibly, still in use. Much of the roof had collapsed, leaving old, rotten timbers strewn everywhere. The far end of the barn was a pile of rubble, but the near end still held its shape, though it looked as if a push with a finger could send it tumbling. A trough lay capsized in the straw on the ground, its wood splintered. To either side, stalls that once housed horses leaned askew.

But one was occupied. A wiry-haired old donkey stood in one of the stalls, its hindquarters to the men. It turned its long head to watch the strangers with one black-pearl eye.

"Well look at you," the deputy said, stepping toward the donkey. "Handsome feller. That crazy old woman was really off her rocker to keep you in this place."

The sheriff shushed him, whispering, "You hear that?"

Jacobs listened, and realized he heard music, thin notes that conformed to no melody. At first, given how they overlapped without rhythm, he thought they might be from a wind chime, but the sound was too continuous, too full of purpose, and somehow beautiful despite its chaos. And the sound, inside the decades-decayed barn, was also somehow frightening.

The trio advanced with the sheriff in the lead. The deputy edged toward the donkey, intending to approach it gently and lead it out. The rooster squawked again, startling them all. For a moment, Jacobs pondered shooting it. It held its ugly head sideways to glare down at them all with one baleful round eye.

The music didn't get any louder. Jacobs looked right and left, up and down, but couldn't pinpoint its source.

"There, there. Easy." said the deputy as he put a hand on the donkey's flank, running his palm across fur bristly as a wire brush.

Standing before a precariously balanced stack of timbers,

the sheriff shined his flashlight over a suspicious-looking mound of straw packed underneath the boards.

The donkey shifted at the deputy's touch, but made no noise. Puzzled, the deputy squinted into the stall, and noticed something lying by the beast's front hooves, clothed in dun and dark brown, the same colors as his own uniform. As the deputy realized what the shape on the floor must be, the donkey kicked him with bone-breaking force.

Neither Jacobs nor the sheriff saw what happened, though both heard a crunch, then a loud crash. They turned to see the deputy lying on his back atop a pile of broken wood, across the barn from the donkey's stall. Then a deafening rumble filled the barn that resolved into a deepest-basso growl. The straw pile that the sheriff had scrutinized erupted.

A jet black mastiff lunged at the sheriff, its mouth extended to reveal teeth like white daggers, its shoulders higher than the lawman's waist.

But Jacobs was distracted by the rooster flapping past him, its talons nearly tangling in his hair. He stared at it in amazement, for its flight was no longer ungainly. Its long wings swooped in a manner impossible for such a bird. As Jacobs stared, he thought for a moment that he saw a completely different form flicker through the air, long sleek legs drawing up, muscled back rippling, a flash of something celestial and malevolent.

The rooster alighted, and the deputy screamed as it pecked his face.

The sheriff shouted too, firing his revolver point blank into the mastiff's muzzle, the gunpowder flashes leaving spots in Jacobs' eyes.

The prosecutor held his pistol out, wavering back and forth between the other two men, stymied as to what to do. Then he noticed the donkey. During the distractions, it had silently sidled up next to him, its huge shaggy head longer than one of his shins.

It was smiling at him. Its lips were stretched along its thick muzzle in a manner that seemed impossible, showing teeth that seemed too large and too numerous, as if a human smile had been carved in some atrocious way into its countenance. The single black eye that met Jacobs' wide-eyed stare sparkled with mirth.

The beast stretched its neck as if it intended to nuzzle. Then it bit down on his arm, and bit through it. The hand holding the gun dropped away to land in the straw.

As Jacobs backed away in pain and shock, a piercing yowl shredded the air, and a dark shape sprang from the rafters. The last thing the prosecutor saw was the blood-flecked donkey's face, still regarding him with one mirthful eye, mouth still stretched in an unnatural, elongated grin. Than a hissing black thing with green eyes and needle claws landed on his shoulders, and the claws took his sight away forever.

With a wail, Jacobs fell.

As his life ebbed away, the bird stopped its attack on the prone deputy, and leapt, wings flapping in great sweeps, to the rafters where the cat had hidden. It opened its beak, and the sheriff distinctly heard words, bellowed loud as a vengeful angel's trumpet:

BRING THE ROGUE TO ME.

The dog stopped growling and stood on its hind legs, as did the donkey, as did the cat.

The sheriff saw three figures, like men, but still beast-like, each baring teeth in unnaturally elongated smiles. The strange music that had tickled the ear so maddeningly when he first came in the barn grew louder, and the air grew darker around the creatures as they started to dance. The dance could have been a simple folk jig, but the smiles of the beings performing it charged each motion with stomach-churning menace. Each raised their arms and turned, and as they did so, they vanished, taking the music with them.

The sheriff, heart pounding, rushed to the stall where the donkey had stood, to discover the musicians had also taken Edward Jacobs' body.

After that, the robbers never dared approach the house again. But the house suited the four musicians of Bremen so well that they did not care to leave it anymore.

Mike Allen is president of the Science Fiction Poetry Association and editor of both the speculative poetry journal Mythic Delirium *and the fantasy anthology series* MYTHIC. *With Roger Dutcher, Mike is also editor of* The Alchemy of Stars: Rhysling Award Winners Showcase, *which for the first time collects the Rhysling Award-winning poems from 1978 to 2004 in one volume. He has poems in* Asimov's, Strange Horizons *and* Talebones, *and stories upcoming in* H.P. Lovecraft's Magazine of Horror *and* Weird Tales. *His newest poetry collections,* Disturbing Muses *and* Strange Wisdoms of the Dead, *are both available from Wildside Press.*

All For a Rose

Donna Quattrone

MY SISTER ALWAYS SPARKLED. She had a thing for baubles and shiny trinkets, glittery nail polish and spangles on her clothes. The boys, of course, were drawn to her. She inevitably had a multitude of invitations to pick from when the weekend rolled around: dinner and a movie or a night out dancing? The house party in the ritziest neighborhood or perhaps a football game with the most popular boy in her class? With a careless flip of her gem-encircled wrist, she'd blithely consider her choices and mark them on her calendar. Her dates would arrive at the door with racing hearts and armfuls of gifts. They'd bring her more trinkets, sweet things to eat and beautiful flowers by the dozen.

I never got them, the boys or the gifts. I had only my father's love and, for a long time, that was enough. My father's love was simple and true and he cared for me well. When he asked what I wanted him to bring back, that last time before his fateful journey, I told him I wanted a rose.

I thought my request would make my sister appear more vain and demanding and foolish. I thought it would show my father that his simple love for me was more than enough. I thought it would feel really good to have someone give me flowers for once.

I thought, I thought, I thought.

What I didn't know was that perfume and trinkets could be purchased on the fly, swept into hip designer bags at duty free shops around the world. What I didn't know was that finding a perfect rose was really quite difficult, and that it would entail a promise that would lead to my father's death. It seems I didn't know much of anything, then.

Father came back from his business trip tired and thin. I thought a round of home cooked meals and a few nights' sleep in his own bed would remedy the situation, but I was wrong again. My sister had a flashy new bracelet and I had a perfect rose. Both of us had a father who was wasting away. It seemed like a bad deal. I didn't know just how bad it was until one night when I heard my father cry out in his sleep. "No," he said, "Anything but that."

I cornered my dad the next morning and pried the story out of him over coffee and Danish. He told me of his search for my rose and of the estate where he had finally found it. He described the perfect petals that had caught his eye because they echoed the blush pink color of spring. He told me of the huge, hairy creature, a frightening beast of a man, who offered to bargain with him. "Send me the first thing that you see when you arrive home," the beast demanded, "And I will let you leave, with the rose, unharmed."

Dad told me how he had laughed as he drove down our street, wondering what it would cost to ship an umbrella stand or a coat rack. Instead, what he saw first was me; smiling in the doorway, waiting for a hug and, of course, my flower. As his tale came to a close, I stared down at my father's colorless face and sad eyes. I held his trembling hand and thought — all this, just for a rose.

The day passed slowly, in a series of options sought, thought out, and discarded. In the end I knew that there was only one path for me to follow. Later that night, I packed my bags. I touched everything I couldn't bring, held all my favorite objects close enough to press a part of them inside me. I slept only a little and woke with a pillow soaked with tears. I tried to be brave at the breakfast table, pretended that the note to my father wasn't wedged in between the daily newspapers and the mail. I held my cheek to his a moment longer than usual before I slipped out the door. And then I found my way to the beast's home.

His house was unmistakable, a gothic monstrosity framed by gardens that hosted a glorious riot of red roses. Every shade was represented in abundance, from the most fragile pinks to the deepest burgundy. The flowers dripped from the doorways and spiraled wildly around the lampposts and trees. They huddled together in shaped clusters or stood proudly in loose groups of blissful color. I stood there, senses overburdened with the mix of sadness and beauty. White-knuckled, I crushed the roses closest to me with both hands and whispered, "I'm here."

"I know," came the rumbled reply. "The bargain is kept."

The beast was, as my father had told me, large and horrible. His tailored suits did little to hide his unwieldy shape. Hair obscured most of his face, and escaped from the top of his shirt and the cuffs of his sleeves. When he gestured for me to follow, I caught a glimpse of huge hands topped off by long, pointed nails. I trailed after him, dizzy from the rich scent of the roses and his overwhelming appearance.

The beast welcomed me to his home and showed me to rooms that, under any other circumstances, would have been splendid. He gave me everything I needed to be comfortable. My favorite gift was a magic mirror that showed me my family. Dad was already starting to feel better and my sister was firming up her dating plans. I'd check in on them regularly; their reflected company was the only connection I had with the world outside of my rose-haunted prison.

As time went on, I became fond of the beast. He was ceaselessly clumsy, his hair was coarse, his features were shaggy and rough, but his manners were impeccable. He painstakingly prepared the most delicious dinners, sumptuous platters surpassed only by the delightful desserts that followed. He brought me roses from his extraordinary garden each and every day, so now I had both sweet things to eat and pretty flowers, always. We'd take long walks and have even longer conversations. At night, the beast would brush my hair and read to me from his vast library of books. He was thoughtful and kind and he cared for me well.

The day came, however, when I looked in my magic mirror and saw only sorrow. My father's illness had returned and my sister had decided she was tired of dating, after all. Their eyes were empty. I knew my place was with the beast, and I knew, because he loved me, that he would honor my request to return home. He asked only that I return in a reasonable amount of time. I left for home that night.

My sister greeted me at the door and I almost didn't recognize her. Her eyes were puffy and her lips were drawn. My dad was in even worse shape. The doctors said there was nothing left to do and it would only be a matter of time, now.

His eyes lit up when he saw me, though. We spent the next few days, my father, my sister and I, holding hands and reminiscing about all the good times we had together. When my father passed on late one night, I knew he went with the comfort of knowing that he had lived and loved well and was loved in return.

Even after the funeral, I didn't return to the beast. I stayed in my father's house and had long conversations with my sister instead. One day, she threw out all her makeup. She spent an entire afternoon on the phone canceling dates and then she ripped her calendar into shreds. She told me that she planned to sell her jewelry and start a memorial fund in Father's name. "I've been looking for love in all the wrong places," she said.

I thought, then, of my beast and of his valentine-colored gardens. I considered promises kept, and broken. I contemplated the security of rose-scented days and long nights of being pampered, and I marveled at the difference between what I thought I was looking for and what it was that I really wanted. I thought about paths followed and of those not taken and all I saw was red, red, red. It was then that I knew I had to return to the beast.

When I arrived at his house, he was nowhere in sight. I found him, eventually, in the very center of his garden. He was motionless, curled into a ball with a single perfect rose clutched in his paw. I put my arms around him and helped him to his feet.

"My love," he whispered, "You've returned."

"Of course," I replied.

He took my hand and said, "This changes everything."

The beast was, indeed, changed. As I nursed him back to health, he became more beautiful each day. Soon he was as sweet on the outside as he was on the inside. One night, as we sat by the roaring fire with fruit and fine cheeses close at hand, the beast told me of the curse, and how I had broken it by returning to him.

"I do love you" I assured him, "But not with the kind of love that will give your story a happy ending. I love you with the kind of love a daughter shares with her father. It's the only kind of love I've ever known." I took a deep breath and continued, "You've given me so much, and for that I am truly grateful, but there is one thing more that I would ask from you now."

Twin tears dropped from his beautiful eyes and ran down his cheeks. "Have I ever denied you anything?" he managed.

I told him what I wished for.

The beast returned, later, feet dragging and eyes downcast, with one brilliant yellow tulip cradled carefully between his fingers. It sat in a vase between us as we ate our supper. I admired the strong, curvy petals that were so very different from the soft shapes and stifling scent of the roses that I'd been surrounded by for far too long.

After dessert, I brought out my magic mirror. I called up my sister's face and passed the mirror over to the beast-turned-beautiful. "She needs a good man," I told him, "And it's about time she started dating again."

He looked at me like I was crazy. Maybe I was. Maybe I still didn't know much of anything. But there was one thing that I knew for certain; I wanted the chance to learn, to experience, to grow. I wanted carousal rides and drive-in movies. I wanted rogue poets and motorcycle boys and wind-in-my-hair adventure. And, most importantly, I wanted choice.

I went around the table and kissed my beast good-by. I would carry my love for him always, but the only thing I took from his house was a single tulip.

It was the color of sunshine. The color of freedom.

Donna Quattrone writes mythic fiction and poetry, does Celtic artwork and is currently discovering that there is life after grad school. (UPENN) She is a native of Bucks County, PA and lives with two feline affection junkies and a multitude of books.

The River in Winter

JoSelle Vanderhooft

THERE IS A REASON WHY I STAY HERE, even when I can't remember it. But when the nights are colder than the North and curled around the edges like the old leaves frozen to my back, I close my wet stone eyes, and memories sweep as surely as old moss along my bed.

The reason comes slowly, sometimes, blue like open sky though the ice above my pale breasts, containing winter, containing silence. My memory is a slippery thing, far more than those of men, wrapped as they are in fog and gusts of snow. When the latticed ice cuts me at its deepest — in the birth-pangs of January — these memories come unbidden. Not many come at first: a river, after all, does not remember much. Just the rustle of a sheet, the careful turning of ankle bones beneath drum-tight skin. Snatches of hair and hands round and soft like old music. A sliver of clouds. A sigh. Not even a name. No, never a name save the thing I am.

And yet there is a reason why I stay here. I am the lady who guards all the algae, the eternal lichens blossoming beneath running water in the spring, still waters in the frost, She who coats each stone and private place with layers of secrets and protozoa. And yet, it was not always so. Once I was a girl with brave fingers. I had a father, several palaces, and gardens of hydrangea and white roses. I wore a diadem upon my brow and danced on feet curved up into glass moons. Then I was young, and careless in the particular and dangerous way that girls are. It was not that I did not mind my steps, no! But that I took so many things for truth: that the moon changed shape with a woman's belly; that questions would be answered if you asked them enough; that thorns could only scratch if you did not look when you reached down to break the stem.

And even, fatally, that men could understand a final no for no.

There were suitors, as any blooming Princess should expect. Skin like sand and skin like sandalwood, they arrived by coach and diamond-bisected hooves, their eyes as many colors as the stones inside the stream that cut the marsh grass underneath my window. Sixteen now, my hips and breasts beginning to meander, my hair unbound like rapids past my waist, I watched their jousts and heard their proclamations. I waited like a statue as they crossed the river's back and ventured through the spindly woods beyond never to return from quests impossible and inhuman — unless it was in a shroud, their colors flying low upon the breeze. Like any blooming Princess I endured this and all things even to the dances. Oh, the balls! By seventeen I had so many gowns — of silver stars, of azure moons, of gold that pierced the sun — that they could not be counted by astrologers' abaci. The gardener, that pale, strange girl from an unpronounceable land, laughed as she stirred the frozen soil with her spade and asked if she could plant them. That way, she smiled, we would have strange and wondrous flowers in April that could outshine the roses and wisteria, and all the lingering snow. Hands in my muffling coat, hair tight about my head I felt the heat rise in my face and wondered why. It was the deadest part of February, when the trees lean upon the fog and even withered leaves seem tired. Surely it could not have been the sun. Yet there were eyes that peered through the grey hedges and the cracks of windows as I slept. And as I breathed and as my body rolled full in womanhood, there was one unfamiliar to old tales.

This was a tall, broad-shouldered guard with heavy hands and eyes. One warm March night when branches swung past the moon as if it had been a-hanging there all season he asked and I said yes, despite myself. My father watched our progress on the floor. And underneath the moonlight and the leaves, the gardener sighed and watched us too, pruning white roses back with steady hands. I saw and felt the breath just beneath my heart. Pressed in the sentry's arms I watched her fingers part the petals, separating death, awakening new life in preparation for the sun. I gasped. He held me hard even as we turned; the gardener-girl flickered through the windows as we danced. Sure as a river spills its banks in Spring, I knew there was importance in the way she bent over the roses with such care; I knew something would change before the Summer, something that made my heart hop in wrists and warmth bloom in my thighs.

But that was long ago. Now I spread the length of this river, rocking in the summer like some great sea cradle, sleeping beneath layers of ice when the world is dark and frogs hide in my intestines. I was once a girl, and there was once a girl who I adored. Now she is gone and I am not. And now it is January, and I lie and dream of fish and feeding time, the spawning that will come in April.

But I am not to be left alone to spread and creep. As the first bubble of January falls from the ice above, she follows. Ice shatters like a stone beneath a hammer and cold water rises; startled, protesting from my sleep I turn as she descends. A thing of burlap and chains, I know she is a woman by her feet — though they are still and numb as dead fish. She falls through cold space into my body and the life sleeping in my secret places. And for me, the thaw comes earlier this year.

I do not know what to do and her body is a heavy line against my breast bone, colder than these remembrances. I had a lover once. What was her name? What did we do? When our sheets wove through her arms and bound her to the bedpost more by accident than design, I laughed. I had lips in those days. They parted with her name as I nipped a rosy shoulder before unbinding her. These chains are harder, but I'm stronger than I was, and they aren't wrapped too tightly. Soon they are off and gone, so is her sheet. Her hair is long and black, and it blossoms like some great anemone in currents churned by her descent. Eyes dark as silt and stones she rises, falls, dancing heavy beneath the cupolas of the ice above.

When I was a girl, before my hair swirled into ripples, I slept in a curtained bed and did not like it. My reed-slim body could not warm the sheets, my toes kicked meters (so it then seemed!) above the corners, useless, cold and lonely. Yet all this was to change.

When Summer raged outside my window all was warm and long beneath the rose-white duvet — hands, legs, hair, fingers locked as if to hold in secrets. Then I lay beneath my gardener. Her breasts were full and hot against my own. I laughed, she smiled. Her back pressed down; like raindrops roll even to a rose's heart, so we met at the center. So heavy, heavy.

Underneath the ice, this woman's heavy. She should drag down, yet her back longs for surface. It should be disturbing, yet I cannot be disturbed, for I have seen too much. I touch her with my hands — ten thousand trails of cilia, green, brown, black. Her shoulders rock, a great bubble bursts from her ragged lips. The stillness falls down like a winter sun, iron heavy, cold and long before its time. The last of the bag tears off and rolls away. She is quite naked, dappled with great bruises — ice marked by maple leaves. She is most curious.

Beware, the ice-bound frogs whisper in my throat. *Don't look at her so closely, or you'll see.* And yet she is so very pale.

And I am heavy in my veins.

I had a lover, once. What was her name? I remember things as cold and deep as ice — a broken mirror, a garden with white roses. In the moon, I saw their veins breathe in and out like the scales of some great fish. Her eyes, so wide and shattered where she fell. The winter of glass blood blooming down my night dress. Beware, the ice frogs whisper in my ears. They whisper in my entrails, and I can feel. They whisper in my ears, and I can hear. They whisper in my nose and I can smell. They whisper in my eyes and I, at last, I can see the rest, but slowly, slowly, for I do not want this past. And with my river's might, that may over-flow a bank and flood a town when the sun is high, I resist.

I think it must be March when all memories return, quick as salmon yearly to their spawning grounds. The ice breaks above me like a mourner, jarring the last pieces into place, and I can fight no more. A little greener now from my embrace, the girl shrinks close as all the frogs awake. I tell them to be quiet as they leave. I've held her for two months and memorized the outlines of candlesticks upon her arms, the angle of her neck where bone met flesh and all breath stopped forever. The bruises down her back give me a map. I trace them, and I know they are the same.

It was July, I was a girl, and so was she. Sitting among the roses I first saw her, passing through the petals silent as the life beneath their leaves. She was so unexpected I thought I dreamed. She turned her head and smiled, and I did not. Some rose bushes had died. She was a gardener, my father's best, sent to make my flowers well again. She had peach lips and hands as soft as rain. I did not look away, and she did not though rapids lashed the pathway to my bed, and all the walls had eyes. She knew her roses well — cut them too deep and they will die. But she knew me better. January yielded slowly to December. I raised my head and shook my petaled hair within my bed chamber, our second garden. I grew up well beneath her in those years. But careful husband though she might have been, she was careless of the eyes that watched by night.

He never meant to enter. He said so later, when I, red and crying, tried to piece again the vertebrae that pierced her flesh. He said he'd heard a noise, the guard whose hands were rough and heavy and eyebrows too attentive. He thought, he said he thought she was a thief. He thought she was another man. At last he said he could not, did not know. Only, I did. Crying God's pardon he closed the sheets and carried her. She leaked heaviness. I screamed. His eyebrows threatened. There was a river. "No one has to know". Her hairline vanished last, like the setting moon, and I was lost.

"No one has to know."

I do not know when I stopped eating. Was it the day his silver armor cut the floor, the day he bought the ring, or the night I pushed and fell, another mouth forcing its way through the river between my legs? Only it lived, and it was screaming. I do not know, I can't recall. I only know that my skin pulled tight, and green, then black, and I became a thing of arms and disease. Soon he, lips dark and vomiting disgust, permitted me to join her.

So many things, but that is all and none. She was not here when I arrived, and yet I stayed. Perhaps in passing, she caressed these rocks as I caress them now.

As I caress this broken corpse that jangles in my arms, beneath the buffering of Spring and thaw.

The ice melts earlier this year, and sure and slow the frogs awake and all the fishes stir. They rise to meet the sun and I turn left and shake my head. And still I hold my burden, this dead girl, knowing she is mine and not, and me. When April comes, the bones grow through her skin. The map is gone, and I must let her go. Clinging to my rocks I watch her leave, a woman-raft of wire and Queen Anne's lace vanishing down the current like a breath.

She is passed, I hug my stones. She is passed through me, through my memories and out into the world and its decay. She is passed, my gardener is passed, and yet I will remain. Somehow — I do not know or do not want to — I could not vanish as this last one did when I melted in this stream. Though flesh and bone, eyes, breasts and hips are washed away a thousand springs ago, my memories will not. And therein lies the question. It has been said the dead may haunt the dead as truly as they haunt a beating pulse, yet what of a ghost who only haunts her memory, sure as the water rises, falls and freezes in the snow?

Remembering, not wanting to remember, I watch her bones meander through the trees.

The frogs begin their song, and deltas, wells and tributaries shake as petals fall. With a roar as heavy as regret, the last ice breaks. Then all is still again.

JoSelle Vanderhooft graduated from the University of Utah in 2004 and has been roaming around the United States ever since. Her first poetry collection 10,000 Several Doors *will be released from Cat's Eye Publishing. She has also edited* Sleeping Beauty, Indeed, *an anthology of lesbian-themed fairytales for Torquere Press (forthcoming May 2006). The coming year will see the publication of several Vanderhooft novels such as* The Tale of the Miller's Daugher *(Papaveria Press),* Vice of Kings *and* Enter Elsinore. *Poetic works can be found in current or forthcoming issues of* Jabberwocky, Sybill's Garage, Mythic Delirium *and* Star*Line. *Online, her fiction can be found at* Reflection's Edge *(www.reflectionsedge.com) and in Issue 1 of* Cabinet Des Fées.

All My Mommies

Virginia Mohlere

I HAVE TWENTY-SEVEN MOMMIES, and they all stay in one room. The are so nice to me, and they tell the best stories. They make me brush my hair and remind me to button up when it's cold. Even though they can't touch me, I know they love me very much. And I think they're beautiful. I don't care what anyone says. I don't mind a bit if some of them haven't got eyes or hands, or if flies crawl out of their mouths, or they drip a little.

The new mommies are usually sad for a while. It's hard for them, because it's so strange. That's what Mommy Besava says, and she was a mommy long before I got here. She's mostly bones now, and her voice is like trying to whisper when your throat is dry. I have to keep very still to hear her. She tells wonderful stories. The shreds of her dress are like the green of a Christmas tree. They are so beautiful that I want to touch them, and even though I know that when I do they'll crumble to dust, sometimes I can't help myself. Then Mommy Besava whispers a shivery laugh.

"Child," she says, "Don't put your fingers in your mouth. You don't know where I've been."

I don't understand the joke. She's been hanging on this wall for as long as I can remember.

Mommy Lizveta is my crazy mommy. I'm so sad for her, because she's always scared, even though the two other mommies who came after her got over being frightened and started telling stories. Mommy Lizveta never tells any stories. She just cries and asks me when I will let her out. I try to tell her that I'm just a little girl, and she says nonononono until I get upset and have to go sit with the older mommies for a while until I feel better. I want to help her, but I don't think she really listens. Sometimes I get so upset that I have to leave the mommies altogether and I go lie down in my bed, squinched down under the covers where it's nice and dark. I'm a big girl now, so I don't do that very often, but when Nurse finds me like that, she makes me a nice posset, and she doesn't scold me at all. Mommy Besava says that Nurse knows about them, but we never talk about it. So it's like the mommies are a secret, but the best kind of secret, because I won't get in trouble if I'm found out, except maybe by Papa.

I hardly ever see Papa. He's always off fighting, or hunting, or getting a new mommy for me. It seems like it takes a long time to get a new mommy. First he has to meet a fine lady, and then he has to woo her. I don't really know what that means, but it's what the books say. I learned how to read two whole years ago. Mommy Angelique taught me, and now I can go into the library and pick out any book I can reach and read it. Papa thought this would mean I could only get to the boring books, but I am a very good climber. I already saw the books with naked people in them. In one of those books, a man with his horn stuck up beats on ladies until their insides spill out. That made me cry until I thought maybe those ladies would turn into mommies. Then I felt better.

I don't have a favorite mommy, but Mommy Angelique is the one who had me, back when she was a lady. I like for her to tell me about it. It's my favorite story. She was a fine lady living in her castle far away, and she had a pony named Jolie who was all brown except for a white star on her forehead. And Mommy Angelique loved her more than anything. She would put on a dress as blue as her eyes (that's what she says: she hasn't got any eyes now) and ride all day. One day she came home and her Papa had a new friend who was the most handsome man she ever saw, with hair as blue as the night sky, and rings on his fingers, and a glint in his eye that made Mommy Angelique think of princesses and adventures and that maybe she wanted to do something more than ride around all day on her pony. That was my Papa, and he stayed in the castle for a long time. He rode out with Mommy Angelique and they went through the woods with beautiful birds on their wrists that hunted rabbits for their dinner. He gave Mommy Angelique jewels and dresses, and he laid beside her in front of the fire and read books of poetry, until she says she was so in love she couldn't see straight, and they got married. She wore a blue velvet dress with a golden silk sash and pearl-tipped pins stuck into her hair and all kinds of people came to see the wedding.

Mommy Angelique says that at the wedding feast, she and Papa danced so much that her shoes filled with blood.

Then they came here to Papa's castle, and lots of the other mommies agree when Mommy Angelique says it's a wild, lonely place. It seems perfectly normal to me, but I've never been anywhere else. Papa stayed here with Mommy Angelique, and they ate fine dinners and rode their horses around. Then I started growing in her tummy, and she was so happy. One day, not long before I was supposed to be born, Papa had to go to the seaside and see about his business. I wish he would take me to the seaside, but he never does. He gave his big bunch of keys to Mommy Angelique, so that she could be in charge while he was gone. Then he pointed to a little rusty key.

"The castle is yours," he said, "except for the room unlocked by this key, at the top of the west tower. Do not go into that room, or I will punish you."

Then he kissed Mommy Angelique and went away. On the first day she looked at the pantries, and all the food laid by. On the second day, she looked at the cellars, filled with potatoes and ever so many bottles of wine. On the third day, she looked at the stable lofts, filled to bursting with hay. On the fourth day, she looked at the galleries, with pictures of people who knew how to stay dead. On the fifth day, she looked at the library, floor to ceiling with books. On the sixth day, she looked at the attics, full of furniture and old papers and dresses. On the seventh day, she looked at the vaults, piled with gold and gems, and she covered herself in jewelry until she felt like a princess.

Then she had nothing to look at, except the room that opened with the little key. She was too big for her horse, so she drove a little cart around the park and thought about the key. The next day it rained, so she read a book and thought about the key. The next day it stormed, so she embroidered my christening dress and thought about the key. The next day was a gale, so she sat by the fire with her hands on her big tummy and thought about that key until she thought her head would burst. She decided that Papa loved her too much to punish her badly, especially with me coming, and that she had to see the room at the top of the west tower.

That's this very room, of course. So Mommy Angelique crept up the stairs, slowly slowly. She said that it was as if the very drafts were tugging at her ankles, trying to pull her back, but still she tiptoed up the stairs. She didn't know that Papa was coming home, galloping galloping through the gale. Up she went, with the little key in one hand and a lantern in the other, her giant belly casting shadows on the wall. Up the stairs and up, with the storm rattling outside and the rust of the little key rubbing on her hand. First the key would not go in the lock, so she had to push it hard. Then the key would not turn, so Mommy Angelique put down her lantern and pulled with both hands, until the key turned and the door opened, even as a great crack of thunder shook the stones.

"I was so frightened that I couldn't breathe," Mommy Angelique says, and I whisper along with her, because I know this story by heart.

The door opened, and the room was as dark as a pit. She picked up the lantern and crept like a mouse over the threshold, holding the light high over her head. It upsets the mommies so, to hear the ladies scream. Mommy Angelique says she screamed until she ripped herself apart, and plop! I fell on the floor. I was screaming too, but just in the way that babies do. Even at that moment, Papa was at the turning of the road, as Mommy Angelique screamed and baby me lay on the floor. And because she was screaming, she didn't know she was bleeding. When Papa was at the gatehouse, the blood was like a pond around me, and still Mommy Angelique screamed. When Papa reached the stables, the blood was a river around me, and Mommy Angelique was starting to fall, her screams like a crying girl. When Papa came in the house, the blood was like a lake around me, and Mommy Angelique made a ragged breathing sound. By the time Papa was at the doorway, the blood was an ocean around me, and Mommy Angelique was silent. Papa looked down and saw that my hair was as blue as his own, so he picked me up and took me down to the kitchens, and the fourth assistant cook became Nurse. Later on he came and hung Mommy Angelique on the wall with the other mommies.

I never needed a key. The door opens at the touch of my hand. As long as I can remember I've been coming here, and Nurse says from the minute I could crawl I was trying to get up the stairs of the west tower. I would be here all day every day, except that it makes Nurse nervous, so sometimes I have to stay downstairs, especially when Papa's home. I got three more mommies after Mommy Angelique, and I'm almost seven years old. Mommy Rosamund, the newest one, is still a little stinky, but that's not her fault. I don't mind it so much. Nurse is teaching me how to knit, and Papa's steward is teaching me sums, but my mommies take care of everything else. Their stories are the best kind of stories. They're very interesting, and at the end, you know something new. I'm learning all the things a fine lady should know: how to keep the silver, where to put the salad forks, how to find out how best to wear your hair, and how to tell when your servants cheat you. None of Papa's servants cheat. I checked. I think they're too scared.

When Papa's home and there's no fine lady, he likes me to sit with him after dinner. I have a little wooden stool that I place at his knee, and he strokes my hair with his big hand and asks about my day. I tell him about reading the boring books in the library, and climbing trees, and helping dig in the kitchen garden. Sometimes I will show him my handker-chief if I did an especially good job with the embroidery. Papa drinks hot wine from a large jeweled cup, and sometimes he will tell me a story when the wine is nearly gone. All of his stories are the same. They're all about bad little girls who get terrible punishments, like the one who lies and gets needles stuck through her tongue or the one who is listening behind the door and her nose gets stuck in the crack when the door opens, so it gets torn off, and she's so ugly after that that she hides in the cellar with the spiders. This is frankly a little irritating, because as far as Papa knows, I am very well behaved. I think he likes to frighten me, so I pretend to be scared, and he kisses me on the top of my head.

"Best to learn this lesson young, child," he says. "Doing what you're told is the key to a long life."

A couple of years ago, when I was very little, one of Papa's stories really did scare me so I told it to the mommies. When they get really upset, they move a little, so their chains clank and their bones rasp together. They were so mad! They made so much noise that I could almost hear them talking outside my head. I remember I thought they were angry at me, and I cried and cried. I was already sad because I thought Papa's story meant that he thought I was a bad girl, so when the mommies got mad, I thought they thought I was bad too. I didn't know where to go, because they were all so angry, and Mommy Lizveta was crying so hard, and I didn't want them to be angry anymore. Mommy Besava hangs next to Mommy Angelique, and that was the day I decided the space between them was my safe spot. I figured that Mommy Besava is very quiet and wise, and I am Mommy Angelique's little baby, so they would get over being mad first. I ran to that spot and sat down, and I put my head on my knees and cried some more.

My mommies can't touch me because they're dead, but sometimes it's like I can feel them in my head. I cried for a little while, and then I could feel their little flutter touches inside, saying, "hush, hush." All the mommies together were saying hush, that it was okay, even my crazy mommy. That made me feel better so fast.

I was glad they weren't angry anymore. They said it wasn't even me they were mad at, but Papa, for scaring me with his story and trying to make me think that little girls were bad. I didn't really understand it then, because I was too little, but that was the first time that the mommies told me how they got to be dead and hanging on that wall: that they had all loved Papa until they couldn't see straight. Then they married him and came here to live, for a week or a month or a year, until Papa went to the seaside and they opened the door and saw the mommies hanging up, all after Papa told them not to and went away. All of the ladies, except for Mommy Angelique, who screamed and bled, saw the mommies and went running downstairs, but the little rusty key got spots of blood on it that wouldn't wash away, so when Papa came home, he could tell. I know now. I have a wicked Papa. He killed all these ladies, his wives, and hung them on the wall. That's why he can tell me stories now about bad little girls and I don't get upset. I would never be as wicked as him.

Of course, it was bad for the ladies to come in the tower when Papa told them not to, but not so bad that he should kill them. So whenever Papa goes away for a long time and comes back with a fine lady for a wife, I'm excited for the new stories, but I feel sad, too, because I know Papa will kill her, and she'll have a rough time until she settles down and realizes that she's dead. I never meet any of the ladies while they're alive, but I bet they were nice. I would like to have a live mommy, who would brush my hair and let me try on her jewelry. I will never have one of those.

My mommies have a plan for me. I know all about it,

because I heard them talking while I stood outside the door. At first I was angry, and I thought they were horrible, so I ran downstairs and spent the day playing in the garden, outside in the wind. All the time I played, I was thinking and thinking. By the time I sat down to my dinner, I had decided that my mommies were right: Papa is a terrible person, and if nobody stops him, he will keep on killing ladies forever. As much as I love my mommies, I don't really want any more. I want them to be able to stay dead and to sleep, especially poor crazy Mommy Lizveta. I want to have friends who are living ladies, and for all the people in my house to not be so scared. I'm too little now, but I'll keep learning and growing and pretending, and when I am big enough, I will make sure my Papa doesn't kill any more ladies. I will plunge that rusty key right into his heart.

Virginia Mohlere lives in southeast Texas with a surfer muse, a cat that eats beans, occasional Wicked Stepchildren and badly organized piles of paper. The ink staining her fingers is green. Neither the snakes nor the lizards in her yard are bothersome, but she has a mortal dread of tree roaches.

Little Red

K. Eason

IT HAD BEEN A FOREST ONCE.

Trees tall as buildings, her grandmother told her. Trees so big you couldn't see the tops.

What happened to them all, Grammie?

And Grammie had made her eyes very big, very wide. *Ah, petite. Progress happened.*

Progress: n. Going on to a higher stage; advance, advancement; growth, development, continuous increase
She wasn't afraid.

Steel and concrete stretched skyward, tangled with neon overhead. Light-bleed and the cloud-bounce and the natural creeping damp made a watery false daylight. But it was night, and somewhere, above skyline, behind clouds, there was a moon. That she knew, even without seeing it. It tugged at her blood with cold round fingers. Appeared behind her eyelids when she blinked, like a lambent inner eye. That was instinct, woven into bone and nerve. Like breathing.

Hunter's moon. She knew that, too.

Not afraid, she told herself again, and picked her way along the narrow asphalt path. Not sidewalk, tonight, and not street — alley, because it was faster, and because tonight speed mattered more.

You must take this bag to Grammie, Mama had told her. *Hurry. Don't stop for anything. For anything, Red. The Rats are moving tonight, and she needs this. Do you hear?*

Yes, Mama.

Grammie came from the original genotype. She needed the drugs to jump the gaps in her biology. But Mama and Red were controlled mutations. Not so vulnerable when clouds hid the moon and the Rats were about.

New and improved, Grammie called them, and slipped the needle into her veins.

Something rustled. She glanced sidelong: just enough street-glow to cut out the rusted silhouette of a dumpster. Full, she noted, of paper and plastic and things that smelled old and organic. The noise repeated itself. A crushed paper cup slid and bounced onto the pavement, splashed into a puddle of something rainbow-slick and dark.

Simple matter, to leave the cup where it had fallen. And yet. She crouched warily. Plucked the cup with careful fingers. Dark crescents smudged the edges, that would be red in real light. Lipstick. She curled her own lip. They never learned.

She tossed the cup back into the dumpster. It slid and skidded along the piles, came to rest on the edge again. Wobbled and held.

Stay, she willed it, and edged a little further into the alley. The building shadows kissed and melted into absolute ink just past the dumpster. Stupid to rush into them, not knowing what might be inside.

Cold sweat and double-thump in her chest. Yet another crackle, and she whipped sideways. Just a rat, of course it was. Except the sweet-rot smell wasn't rat. Not just.

Are you afraid to go alone? Almost mockery, in Mama's moon-pale stare, as she'd draped the bag's strap across her shoulders.

And dry-mouthed, damp-palmed, the lie she meant to make truth. *No.*

Stretch of shadow-black just in front of her. She adjusted the bag on her shoulder again. Not heavy, just awkward: too-long strap that bumped against her hip and thigh when she walked. Packages inside, soft-sided lumps pressing out against the canvas. She pulled it around and cradled it against her belly and stepped into the opaque dark. One, two, three steps. Four. Steel bands constricted around lungs and heart. Her throat felt too small.

The sweet-rot stink got bigger, took on its own shape. Rat-like, if rats grew as big as crocodiles and had red LED eyes. She imagined the whisper-slide of claws on the asphalt. Heard a leathery whisper, then a bang. The dumpster groaned and creaked as metal buckled. Not rat, but Rat.

She froze.

Who's afraid now?

She imagined Mama's sharp-edged smile.

Cancer: n. A malignant growth or tumor that spreads indefinitely and reproduces itself, as also tends to return after removal; it eats away the part in which it is situated, and generally ends in death.

The Rat hissed. Rocked up onto its haunches. As tall as her now, and wider. It locked eyes. Pointed yellow teeth at her and sniffed a scabrous nose. Their people and hers were old enemies. Parallel evolution, predator and scavenger together. Rats hadn't bothered with engineering: had sought any change at all and counted it improvement, no matter the effects.

"Little wolf," it murmured. "Little *lone* wolf."

Ice and wire tangled in her belly. She scanned the roofline for pitch and shadow silhouettes and red pinspot eyes. Listened for skittering claws.

Nothing. Yet. Rare to find just one Rat. They lived in colonies. Networked, so that what one saw, the others did. Vermin, parasite, prey. She should not talk to it. Should run.

She would be faster than the Rat: be through the alley and on the street before it could catch her.

A part of her rebelled: insisted that *she* should not be the one to run.

Once upon a time, petite, we took the small and the weak and sick. When we can, we still do.

Nothing small or weak about the Rat. But sick, yes, it was that. They all were. This one had patchy fur striped with ooze, one ear missing, one of its eyes pulsing pink.

Don't stop for anyone. For anything. Do you hear?

But Mama hadn't known about the Rat. And there was only one. She could handle *one*.

She straightened. Eased the bag around her body so its weight sat at the base of her spine. Flexed her fingers. They felt cold, contrast to the flush-heat in her cheeks, to the full-auto ache in her chest. Felt like bones might split and spill her heart into the alley.

Are you afraid?

Yes.

She worked her hand up slowly, reached for her pocket. Forced herself to talk like Mama, low and slow and fierce. Told her hands not to shake. "I'm not alone, vermin."

"No?" Red-beam scanned from LED eyes, sweep and return. The left one beat like a heart. "I only see *one* of you."

Her hand crept a little further up her jacket, poked inside the open flap. Found cool metal and wrapped around it. She pulled the gun out, one motion, and pointed it like Mama had taught her. Locked onto the single solid glow in the Rat's matted face.

"Good eye," she said, and shot him in it.

She expected squealing, thrashing, maybe blood. Got a slow topple instead, hollow thump when it landed. Gunshot echoes off the bricks. Silent seep of something dark and thick onto the pavement. The tail wormed around blind for the thirteen seconds. She counted them — *one one-thousand, two one-thousand* — until it stopped. Mostly-quiet flooded back and spread solid. Distant noises leaked in around the edges. Slivers of sound, human and machine whispering together in a cybernetic conspiracy.

She broke the post-mortem hush: her own breath catching up, heaving out of her in a rush. She took a step with knees that shook and glanced down at the Rat. Told herself the glow in its remaining eye was reflection, imagination. Nothing but the last sparks in a failing system. She knelt anyway. Pressed the gun into the hollow under the Rat's ear and fired. Muffled bang.

This time, the light went out.

Stop for nothing, Mama had said, and she'd stopped too long already. Made too much noise. No telling how many other Rats had caught this one's dying upload. How many were mapping their way to this alley. More than she had bullets, anyway. She could not stay.

But I killed it. Only one Rat, and still. Mama would be proud of that. Grammie would. She thought of Grammie's face, her smile, when she heard what Red had done. Wouldn't mind that she'd delayed. That she was late.

Very, very late.

She stood and lasered a glance down the alley. No more shadows. No Rats. Nothing but neon-splash on the street ahead, rainbow smears of viscous damp. And overhead — overhead, she felt the moon moving. Poking rusty orange through the cloud-veil. Climbing.

She had to hurry. She gulped the urban sour into her lungs and worked herself into a lope.

* * *

Evolution, n.: When pertaining to biological organisms and processes, the process of developing from a rudimentary to a mature or complete state

Grammie lived in the heart of the city. A park, Mama said. Once upon a time, anyway. Now it ran feral, sullen shrubs and ragged lawns. Grass trespassed the concrete borders, competed with weeds for space in the cracks. Tried to bury the little bare-scuff path that snaked off the sidewalk and back into the trees.

She stopped and panted and caught breath. Popsicle streetlights melted yellow on the sidewalks. She leaned against one. Squinted past the border of the light. Couldn't see the house from here. It had been a caretaker's cottage, something small and unassuming and meant to slide away from the casual glance. Now it hid itself utterly, ringed in shadow and forest.

She patted the bag again. Felt the gentle bulges, heard the quiet *tink* of glass. Nothing broken. Another once upon a time, what she carried would've been contraband. Still might be, if anyone cared. But other concerns took precedence now. Survival. Adaptation. Predator, prey, scavengers on the fringes.

One of the streetlights buzzed. Flickered. Sizzled dark as she watched it. Its neighbor followed suit, and the one after it — *one one-thousand, two one-thousand* — as if on a timer. Planned deaths in sequence. But the lights lived on the city grid, which would mean

rats

a cascading overflow on the system. Could be a random overload. Could be, except there had been only one Rat in the alley, and Grammie was already sick, and Red wasn't supposed to stop for anything. Grammie's house wasn't on the grid. Wasn't open to swarms or spies from the uplink, but they knew. Somehow. Sensed the vulnerability.

We take the weak and the sick, Grammie said, *but we aren't the only ones.*

Red found the path from habit. Hurried along as fresh dark spread along the sidewalk behind her. The bag banged against her hip until she gathered it up against her belly again. Cradled it there in one arm and thrust the other ahead. Grass scraped aside as she ran, whispered against her boots. Branches batted higher. Gouged her bare arms bloody. Ozone stink competed with fresh copper, with something that reminded her of Rat and wasn't. Not entirely.

Grammie.

Last bend in the path, last rake of talon-branches, and she was there. Small clearing, weeds in riot, little cottage locked up dark. The clouds spread out overhead, low and smoky. Solid. Ancient Christmas lights peeked past the drawn curtain-shrouds. Spangles of color leaked through the gap between door and jamb.

The door was open. And Grammie never, ever left it like that.

She's expecting me. But Red stopped anyway. Swept her gaze on a circuit of the clearing. Saw nothing in the weeds, nothing moving. No LED eyes. Heard nothing, either, except the static murmur of Grammie's old radio. She licked her lips and dashed across the open. Tucked up against the wall beside the door. Reached a hand across the gap and rapped a knuckle on the peeling wood.

Once. Twice. She jerked her hand back and fisted it against her thigh.

"Red?"

And that sounded like Grammie. Red closed her eyes. Breathed deep. Sweet-rot smell. Stank like plague, like the

Rats, except the whole city did. Grammie had it, too. Slow death that the old ones always got after a lifetime of resistance. Genetic failure at the end, system worn

weak and sick

smooth with fighting and the drugs that forced the change. Red and Mama might not get the plague. Might not. If they lived that long.

"Red, is that you?" Sharper now. Movement inside, thumps and scrapes. Could be Grammie's joints gone stiff and awkward. Could be

vermin

something else. Coming closer now, whatever it was. She felt vibration through the wall at her back. Solid. Heavy steps. Weight behind them. And Grammie wasn't a big woman.

Red opened her eyes wide. Let her pupils gather up the darkness. No bleed from the street now, no moon through the overcast sky. Only the crack of light coming out of the cottage through the open door. The world resolved itself in soft edges and shades of black. She imagined she saw pin spots of red ringing the clearing. Imagined she heard bodies moving in the trees. Smelled only sweet-rot. Felt her skin ripple and bristle. Battle-instinct. She damped it back. *Not yet.* Took a careful glide-step away from the wall, back from the door.

"Red! Answer me!"

Her chest turned solid. Right accent, but too sharp on the edges for Grammie. Too crisp for plague-scarred lungs. Recorded, processed, digital. Something broad and dark eclipsed the wedge of light, squeezed the clearing down to pitch. And it was far, far too big to be Grammie.

She ducked a shoulder and slid the strap over it. Set the bag down carefully. Jumped back as the door swung wide. Another smell crept out below the sweet-rot: thick and metallic, copper-sharp. It pooled in her throat and stuck there. Blood. Far too much for something living. She'd come too late.

We take the weak and the sick.

But so did the Rats. They'd gotten Grammie, and now they meant to take her, too.

But I am neither weak nor sick.

Somewhere overhead there was a moon. Swollen, orange Hunter's Moon. Enough to save Grammie, if she had seen it. If the clouds had let it through. But they hadn't, and Grammie had been only a woman when the Rats came. Old and weak and sick and alone. But Red didn't need to see it. She felt it overhead and inside at once, through blood and bone and nerves. She took the moonlight in her bones and twisted it. Spat it out again and rode the change. Clothing shredded. She stepped away from the metal thump of the pistol as it landed. Flexed claws. She didn't need a gun now.

Behind her the cottage door creaked and moaned. Splintered outward as a body crashed, impatient, against stiff hinges. Not her imagination now, the ring of watching eyes. Or the mutter of grass under too many paws. She bared her teeth and snarled.

Are you afraid?

No, Mama. Not anymore.

The Rats swarmed. She surged to meet them.

It had been a forest, long ago. Trees tall as buildings. Trees so big you couldn't see the tops. Wolves had hunted there, once.

Wolves still did.

Kat Eason is a recent transplant to Southern California, where she lives with a graduate student husband, two black cats, and a great many books. She writes obsessively, paints occasionally, and drinks a lot of coffee in the meantime.

Owls

Maria Beliaeva

AT THE EDGE OF THE WOOD, two owls. From within dark foliage, they peer at each other with their round, round eyes. With the same eyes, they look upon the other wood. The concrete wood of stooping buildings with their hollow windows. Windows staring back at the owls with the same round stare.

It was their wood once. The owls'. But they don't live there now, though sometimes, at night, they might fly into that other wood and look for something. Food perhaps, though they have plenty of that. Perhaps, also, they resent the men who took over their trees. But we can't be sure. They're only owls after all.

Also, in that concrete wood of stooping buildings and crooked telegraph poles, there lives a girl by the name of Masha. That's for Maria. Girl is subjective, too. At the time we're talking about, she is barely sixteen, but she isn't a girl. Couldn't be farther from it. Masha doesn't go to school, she lives with Katerina Pavlovna, her mother, in a small room in a communal apartment. Nothing too shabby there. That's because Katerina Pavlovna is a market woman. She sells fruits and vegetables at the market. Masha isn't quite sure where she gets them from, but there is always a lot of Azerbaijani talk around Katerina Pavlovna. Masha helps Katerina Pavlovna at the market and they are never too hungry, because they are the ones selling the food.

When they are back from a day's sale, Katerina Pavlovna goes to the communal kitchen and makes soup while Masha sits in their room. She likes their room best of all. Between the two red rugs, one on the floor, one on the wall, a window shines blue-white. Just an illusion: when you step closer it is grey. Masha sits at the chipped windowsill and watches the endless dirt of roads and wrecks below. And drab figures, shadowed forms against the grey, crawling slowly through like ants under a monstrous weight. Masha and her mother live on the third floor, but the bicycle shack is just below. It is so crooked you could climb up on it if you wanted, and then, you'd stand just opposite Masha's grey window.

"Masha?"

"Yes, Mama?"

"Who was that you was talking to?"

Masha looks back at the window. He's gone.

"No one."

"Don't no-one me, you little hussy!"

Masha gets up, walking carefully past her mother to the corridor.

"We'll see, Masha. We'll see."

Who was Masha talking to? That's no big secret. Except for Katerina Pavlovna, of course. Every evening, Masha received a visit from a certain Fedia Sokolov. That's for Fedor. They both knew better than tell Katerina Pavlovna. Fedia had a reputation of his own. He'd been around, or so they say. But that's not what appealed to Masha. She couldn't even explain it to herself. Except that Fedia, in all his crassness, his absolute unreliability, his very visible frailness, was very much like herself. He had something of the bird. Not a metallic, mechanical bird. Not a toy. A real bird, such as were almost forgotten. As if, somewhere within Fedia, there was still that wild thing that Masha missed sometimes when walking through the town, though she had never known anything else, being born and raised within cement walls.

They didn't do much when they saw each other. They

only talked. Of trivial things, too, such as their lives, and other people's. No dreams, no futures, no plans. How could they speak of things neither had thought about?

And then came the day when Fedia didn't come. Masha waited at the window, searching the darkness for his winged silhouette. Fedia had a long winter coat that flapped about him like the wings of some grim raven. But, that time, he didn't come. That's when Katerina Pavlovna came in behind Masha and put a stiff hand on her shoulder.

"He won't be coming back, your flighty friend."

"Why?"

"I turned him in. Him and his unholy habits and his band of dirty buddies. We've enough druggies as it is, around here."

Masha looks around, out the window, at the orange darkness of the lighted streets. At the real darkness of the woods beyond. Far away, the woods. And Fedia, farther still.

The wolves, of course, are the first step.

Bones poking through their threadbare shirts, bulbous veins, gaunt, unshaven faces. And smells of booze and cigarettes and other unholy things. But, sometimes, you can't afford to be holy. The wolves' teeth are always bared in a leer of outraged anger. Masha is scared of the wolves.

Grey wolf, cunning wolf, don't bite my hand,
I come not as prey but as friend.

"You want to find Fedia, do ya?" asks the youngest.

They're always like that, the youngsters of the pack. Quick to ask. Quicker to bite. Quickest to be bitten.

"Yes," she says, and looks from her slush-covered boots to the crack in the wall.

That's the thing with them. You have to avoid eye-contact. They're wolves, after all.

"You're that Masha ho, aren't you?" he yapps and

Masha nods.

"I'll go get Grey."

That'll be the leader. Masha's guess, as always in such matters, is correct. The Grey Wolf is greyer and meaner than the rest of them. His hairy arms are covered in cross tattoos. The death mark. Nothing to be scared of, though. After all, if he's killed that many already, he's bound to be picky. Masha isn't the prey his kind look for. Just a glance at her is enough.

"Fedia..." he sucks on his cigarette, "Fedia's gone."

Masha looks up. For the first time, she meets the wolf's blue gaze. A golden fang glistens beside a dark gap. But Masha looks on because that's the only way.

"The fairy's got him," mutters the wolf.

And again, Masha looks away. This time, not because she's afraid of the wolf, but because she's heard of the fairy. The merciless fairy that hugs men in claws of steel, never to release them again.

"Where is he?" she asks.

Another puff of smoke.

"You'd better ask the bears."

Between iron spikes, the streetlights diffuse their sickly orange halos where the last snows melt to a vomit-like muck. Distant factory chimneys exhale clouds of black smoke, beneath them, tramways rattle along a slippery track. Car carcasses, slushed over, lay like dead ships on their sides while rust eats at their once chromed steel. A drop in the puddle of black rainbows and the smell of gas, nothing more, nothing less.

A dark shadow creeps past. A gypsy. But Masha has nothing worth stealing, so she smiles and the woman stops. Also a girl. A woman-girl like Masha. Maybe younger too, judging from her insolent smile and her quick, silent feet.

"He's gonna kill me for it, but here you go."

With a rustle, something green wedges its way into

Masha's palm.

"Your sweetie got taken by the fairy, didn't he?" she whispers.

"Yes," says Masha.

"Mine too. I hope you find him."

And in a patter of naked feet she's gone.

"Thank you," sighs Masha.

She almost pities the girl. That was her day's robbery. She'll get a thrashing, all right.

"Go check with the bears. They take care of the fairy's victims fine," answers a voice from the shadows.

If anything, the bears are more frightening than the wolves. Sure, wolves are unpredictable and mean. Mean to the bone. But at least, they're fair. Unto a measure, that is. As in, they won't strike unless they feel they need to. They always have a reason. Not so the bears. Masha shudders, tripping across the dirt towards the nice part of town. Once more, nice is relative.

"Where you going, broad?" asks the bear at the entrance.

He wears a three-piece suit, dark glasses and a golden ring which he uses to grind the passing wolves into a pulp. Not only the wolves. That's the scary part. Bears, they don't care. They strike because they want to. Masha sighs as the bear motions her forward. Lucky, lucky, lucky.

Master Bear, Master Bear, let me come into your lair,
Master Bear, I pray be kind, I have only good in mind.

"Fedor Sokolov?" the Master Bear gives a powerful yawn, "I have no idea . . . "

"Thank you for your time," whispers Masha.

Quickly, quickly, she presses the dollars into the expecting paw.

"Now, let me think," he grumbles, "We had him on file,

didn't we?"

Masha closes her eyes. She has no more dollars.

"Three months ago. Theft. Mild delinquency. Not much, not much."

She opens her eyes again, and sees the bear frown. He's thinking. Lucky, indeed.

"Yes we got a complaint, yesterday. But... No, we don't have him."

With a grateful sigh, Masha turns to leave.

"Try the morgue," finishes the bear, turning back to his newspaper.

But the bear didn't mean the real morgue, the one that's under the town hospice. Masha knows what the bear meant. The morgue that is the fairy's kingdom. Where she loses her victims in an endless forest of sharp needles and sleepless dreams.

Ankle-deep in the clay, Masha walks. And treacherous as ever, her heart quickens in an unplanned excitement. The dark wall of the old wood stands before her and it's almost as if she can't wait to go in. You have to be crazy to want to got there. You really do. But Masha doesn't mind. All she sees are the endless rows of pure darkness. Not the dirty orange darkness of the town, but something real. Something more frightening than the meanest wolf, the strongest bear ... And at the same time, something like home. At least that is what Masha feels, as she steps carefully among the scattered branches into the other wood.

Contorted oaks, birches frozen in mid-swoon, drab ferns, collapsing trunks, their peeled-off bark sticks out in deadly spikes. Between the weedy soil, sometimes, the surreal splash of color of some misplaced flower. In nooks hidden from view, the turf is dappled with blue forget-me-nots, hazed-over by luminous cobwebs.

Red mushrooms cover mossy stumps with their blood-colored caps. Sometimes, a patch of knotted roots might yield a lonely stone.

On Masha walks and above, between the tight-knit branches, the sky grows pale. An eerie mist of cold wetness and then, a clearing. In its middle a house. But a house such as she's never seen before.

Lopsided and wooden, it stands on two thin pillars, as if expecting to be drowned in the mists.

Little hut, chicken-legged hut! Turn your front to me and your back on the wood.

"Pah! Who's this?" sniffs the hag inside.
Masha walks in, and bows to the witch. Scaly skull, matted grey hairs and crooked nose. A dress of patches and holes, a mean laugh in her beady eye.

"Good morning, Grandma. I am searching for my Fedia."
"Fedia?" cackles the witch, "The fairy's got him, all right."
"But where can I find him, Grandma?"
"That I will tell you, my beauty, if you work for me and do my bidding for seven days."

Masha nods. The witch makes her drink, makes her eat and puts her to sleep.

All through the next week, Masha works for the witch, helping her pull the weeds in her earthen garden, herding her boars in the neighboring clearings, pulling the water from the hidden spring. And all through the week, Masha hears the wild shrieks of the fairy dancing about the misty wood.

After the week has passed, says the witch to Masha:

"Go out to the deepest part of the wood, marked by the oldest, tallest oak, where only owls eyes can see clear. There, you will hear the fairy singing. Listen to her cries and they will lead you to your Fedia."

"Thank you, Grandma," says Masha.

89

"I wouldn't bother if I were you," croaks the witch, "The fairy likes a dead man's dance. She says bodies swing better dead than living."

With those ghastly words in mind, Masha follows the path to the heart of the wood, where devil's mushrooms grow in circles and owl's eyes shine golden in the branches. There, she hears the fairy shriek and sees the hovering shapes of the dead dancers. Their ghosts float tired from their last wild waltz, but still restless as they yearn for more.

A gasp and Masha hides behind the oak. On the other side, the fairy flies and Fedia follows as best he can. His weary legs, his arms, his all too human head weigh him down, but he dares not abandon. In a multicolored haze of leafless wings and metallic heels the fairy swirls, grabbing at his hands with long, cold fingers. The fire of her flailing hair singes his cheeks and they take off together in a whirlwind of acid-colored clouds. Only when he feels her sharp fingernails digging once more into his arm does Fedia breathe again.

"Oh Fedia, my Fedia!" cries Masha.

She leaps to where his body has fallen, limp in the crook of a bulbous root. The fairy is nowhere in sight.

"Fedia, Fedia, can't you hear me?"

But firmly, he shuts his eyes and deeper yet, he sleeps.

And under his shut eyelids, Fedia sees the fairy, in all her splendid toxic beauty and her bewitching fires. And he thinks he loves her more than life itself, because the fairy flows through his veins and her acrid smell coats his thin nostrils and strips away his wings.

A rippling wind blows through the ferns and the fairy sings once more her deadly song.

"Give me back my man, you thief!" cries Masha, as the fairy dances, "Let him go! Let him go! Let him go!" she howls wolf-like into the trees.

And suddenly, the fairy stops. She glances about, her

fawn eyes wider than saucers. Masha looks around too. Somewhere, far in the mists between the endless trees, a solitary howl answers. Slowly, slowly, other throats pick up the lonesome call. The wolves. The lost ones, suddenly awakened from their fairy-induced torpor by Masha's human howl. And perhaps, in their savage wolf minds, in their trapped forgotten souls, they remember who and what brought them there. The fairy with her gauzy fingers rippling in the wind, and her flighty heart that now beats louder than thunderstorms.

And on and on, the lonesome, angry cry is called into the woods, and closing in on the fairy captor that is their captive now, they lock her in a cage of trees and howls and leaden hearts. And they rip her to shreds, in their own craving for more toxic fairy blood. And soon enough, there is no fairy left, except some poisoned drop between two golden fangs.

"Fedia!" a heart-wrenching shriek and suddenly, he jerks awake.

But instead of the fairy's eyes he sees Masha's tear-stained face.

"Where . . . " he murmurs, "Fairy?"

"I chased her off, Fedia. I've set you free."

And she shows him his scarred, bruised arm where the fairy dug her fingernails, and the broken bottles where the fairy's blood had been, and the poison that had been the fairy herself, and in the mists that stretch across the trees, the haggard backs of the phantom wolves that had once been the fairy's captives, too.

"I thought you didn't want me," says Fedia, as he touches Masha's face with a trembling hand.

"Who really wants you, Fedia? The one who lured you away into a dance of death? Or the one who walked across wood of concrete and wood of trees, who bargained with wolf and bear and witch to get you back?"

* * *

With his winged coat once more on his back, and her light step returned to her weary feet, Fedia and Masha walk back to the town where birds like them belong. They wish they could remain in this eternity of real trees and feathers, unscathed by the town's black fumes. But reason tells them to go, and the cold mists urge them off as round-eyed owls click their dark beaks in warning.

And with each step Fedia and Masha take, their wings grow mistier and their bond tamer. It is still there, of course, that bond that only sacrifice can weave. But as they near the grim-faced buildings with their bleak, empty eyes, their steps fall more squarely on the ground. And with a certainty of destiny well-planned in its outlines of chalk, they walk back to their lives suddenly full of futures.

Happily ever after. And once more, life is a boredom that stretches boundless and grey. And once again, only the owls, still hidden in the trees, remember what to seek and whom to resent. They're only owls, after all.

———

Maria Beliaeva, 18 years old, is a Russian-born freelance writer. She has lived most of her life in Paris, France, where she completed her secondary education with a Baccalauréat in Literature with mention très bien (highest honors). She has now moved to Canada to pursue her post-secondary education in English Literature. She has collaborated with the French publications Je Bouquine *and* Telerama. *Her English poetry had been published in the American magazine* Potluck *and in e-zines* Tamafyhr Mountain Poetry, Exquisite Death *and* Descending Darkness. *Her fiction has been published in e-zines* Bewildering Stories *and* Dark Krypt.

In the Woods

Máire NicAodh

In the woods
Love will perish
With the frost.

SHE MET HIM IN SUMMER.

The day was hot, still, and the pollen motes hung like a golden breath in the green light.

It was deep in the woods: beyond the path, past the ancient mound of stone where the shadows lay thick, and beside the lake of shivering rushes.

His blood tainted the clear waters pink.

She pulled him, dripping, onto her lap. His strange blue eyes looked up into hers . . . and it was done.

It was forbidden to take home one such as he. Futile, she was told.

"He will not thrive here," her father warned, his hand heavy upon her shoulder, and concern etched into his seamless face.

She shook off the advice, and the hand, and tended to the man with the grievous wound.

Desperate, she sang to the heart of the forest, glimmering in moonlight, and begged for his survival.

He cannot stay, but he will live.

She bowed her head at the judgement, and her tears splashed on his fevered face.

That night he groaned and twisted as she sat by his bed

and wiped his sweating brow with a cool cloth.

"Marry me," he whispered, his eyes bright and unfocused, "come live with me." He gripped her hand with pain and ardour, and she squeezed back.

"I will," she breathed.

"You will not!"

The boy's face, pale from recuperation and too-early travel, flushed pink. He inhaled carefully, trying not to wince at the effort.

"She saved my life. I love her."

His mother laughed, amused by her son's naïveté, but she noted the determination in his clenched fist, and his erect stance despite the tremble in his legs.

She swept him, protesting, into a chair by the fire, and brewed him a tonic while he spoke of his graceful woman of the woods, whose voice guided him back from the land of shades.

Later, as her son slumbered from the effects of her potion, the dame hummed an off-key tune and spiders crawled out of deep crevices and shunned tunnels to weave a web of enchantment under the moonless sky.

The next morning as she greeted the woman she had chosen to marry her son she draped the dark cobwebs over her face.

"For luck," she explained at the young lady's grimace.

When the boy woke up, groggy, his first sight was of the beautiful maid on his mother's arm.

He forgot the woods.

He forgot the sweet voice that stayed death.

He forgot the promise made to the girl on the summer's night.

By evening his mother toasted the engagement of her son. The village buzzed about the adoration in his eyes, and the young woman's attractive dowry.

Summer faded and autumn ripened. Scarlet berries clung to bare branches sparkling with frost.

The wedding day dawned, crisp and clear. The smell of roast pig and goose, baked potatoes, and pies bursting with fruit filled the wedding hall. The last vines of summer were twisted around the doorway for luck.

At dusk the bells rang out, and the hot hall was packed with well-wishers. The couple, crowned in silver, were handsome and happy. It was a true love match, the village decided.

Each person approached the newly-weds with a gift and a blessing; to their left the groom's mother kept tally.

Last in line was a veiled stranger. When no one else was left the lace was cast off to reveal a young woman, clad in a gown of forest leaves, whose auburn hair was caught in a golden mesh. She stepped up to the laughing couple.

The boy's mother started at the sight of her, and attempted to rise. One look from the woodland maid silenced the mother forever: her feet took root, her throat was blocked, and bark grew over her skin. No one noticed her sudden stillness as all attention was upon the beautiful stranger.

A hush descended. The whisper of the woman's gown was the only sound as she moved closer to the couple.

She reached forward and wiped the groom's brow and eyes with a cool cloth. The enchantment fled.

He remembered the woods.

He remembered the sweet voice that stayed death.

He remembered the promise made to the gentle girl on the summer's night.

"One kiss is all I ask," she said, "and then I will leave."

The new bride, confused and unhappy, did not know how to object.

The husband stood and kissed her, slow and long, as the town watched in shocked silence.

Afterwards, the woman turned, and left the hall. A trail of dying leaves marked her path.

A scream broke the silence as the mother's transformation was noticed—leaves budded from her hair, and the floorboards beneath her ripped and bucked as roots burrowed down and deep.

The bride grasped her husband's arm, and he turned to look at her with eyes clouded with confusion.

"My love, my love," she pleaded.

"Who are you?" he whispered.

Born in the USA, and raised in Ireland, Máire writes the mutated fiction of her dreams. She completed a M.A. in Screenwriting in Sept 2005. Her website is: http://splinister.com

H.G. Wells in Fairyland

Nick Freeman

'Yes,' he said, '"fairies" certainly strike a little
curiously on the ear in these days.'
   Arthur Machen, 'The Shining Pyramid'
   (Machen, *Horror* 9)

Introduction: Forwards or Backwards?

At first sight, H.G. Wells seems unlikely to be sympathetic
towards the fairy story. A scientist and rationalist with
radical political views, he was allied with many 'progressive'
currents in English culture in the years before World War I.
Until his optimism was rudely punctured by the horrors of
that conflict, Wells looked forward to the twentieth century,
believing that the post-Victorian world would see technology
improve human life, and that enlightened mankind would
embrace a new era of sexual equality. Unlike those pessimists
catalogued in John Lester's *Journey through Despair* (1968),
Wells saw the ending of the Victorian period as a cause for
celebration. Why then did he greet its Edwardian successor
with 'Mr Skelmersdale in Fairyland', first published in the
London Magazine in February 1903 and reprinted in *Twelve
Stories and a Dream* later that year? Surely by 1903 the fairy
story was far too associated with the Victorian past to appeal
to a forward-thinking writer such as H.G. Wells?

Fairies had been enormously popular in Victorian
England. 'The Victorians desperately wanted to believe in

fairies,' argues Christopher Wood, 'because they represented one of the ways they could escape the intolerable reality of living in an unromantic, materialistic and scientific age' (Wood 8). Fairies appeared in 'illustration, literature, poetry, theatre, ballet, and music' as well as in what Wood terms 'the golden age of fairy painting' between 1840 and 1870 (11). By the late nineteenth century, they were also, as Diane Purkiss reminds us, staples of children's fiction and art (Purkiss 247-64), and in many ways had been stripped of the erotic aspects that they had possessed in earlier incarnations, such as the paintings of Henry Fuseli (253). By writing a fairy story, Wells could be seen to be associating himself with attitudes he had elsewhere done much to oppose. In his early fiction, science, if not materialism, offered all manner of romantic possibilities, while in his recent work the realities of sexual feeling were demanding ever more urgent expression. By 1903, Wells had published a number of short stories, as well as *The Time Machine* (1895), *The Island of Doctor Moreau* (1896), *The Invisible Man* (1897), and *The War of the Worlds* (1898). He had also begun to venture beyond the confines of 'scientific romance' with the autobiographical *Love and Mr Lewisham* (1900), and was working on another story of lower middle class life, *Kipps*, published in 1905. In short, he was both the world's premier writer of what would become 'science fiction' and an increasingly respected 'serious' novelist, the friend of Henry James and George Gissing. It is undoubtedly surprising to see him publishing a fairy story, especially one that is apparently so traditional in form and detail, but 'Mr Skelmersdale' is rather less innocent than it first appears.

* * *

Reading 'Mr Ŝkelmersdale'

The story begins with the unnamed narrator, a re-searcher into 'Spiritual Pathology' (Wells 884), going to a village in Kent to work on a book. Here he meets Skelmersdale, a grocer's assistant who is mocked by the other villagers after claiming to have spent three weeks in Fairy-land ten years before. Initially reluctant to tell his tale, he finally confides in the narrator, describing how 'possibly on Midsummer Night', he had an argument with his intended, Millie, and walked up to Aldington Knoll, glossed by the narrator as 'an artificial mound, the tumulus of some great prehistoric chieftain' (889). Here he fell asleep and 'vanished for three weeks from the sight of men', returning at last with 'his cuffs as clean as when he started' and 'his pockets full of dust and ashes' (886).

During his time in Fairyland, Skelmersdale was courted by the beautiful Fairy Lady, who 'sat on a bank beside him in a quiet secluded place "all smelling of vi'lets," and talked to him of love' (892). However, he refused to abandon Millie, and announced his ambition to amass 'enough capital to open a little shop' (892), with the result that the Lady took him to a cavern filled with coffers. Here she left him, saying that the gnomes who lived there would reward him with fairy gold. Realising he had lost her, Skelmersdale rejected the precious metal in despair and fled in search of her:

> So he ran [. . .] out of this red-lit cave, down a long grotto, seeking her, and thence he came out in a great and desolate place athwart which a swarm of will-o'-the-wisps were flying to and fro. And about him elves were dancing in derision, and the little gnomes came out of the cave after him, carrying gold in handfuls and casting it after him, shouting,

'Fairy love and fairy gold! Fairy love and fairy gold!'

And when he heard these words, came a great fear that it was all over, and he lifted up his voice and called to her by her name, and suddenly set himself to run down the slope from the mouth of the cavern, through a place of thorns and briars, calling after her very loudly and often. (895)

The denizens of the fairy world pursued him into a swamp, where he tripped over a twisted root and found himself sprawled upon Aldington Knoll once more, 'all lonely under the stars' (893) like one of W.B. Yeats's love-struck speakers in *The Rose* (1893) or *The Wind Among Reeds* (1899). Three weeks have passed, and his absence has caused Millie to turn against him: she marries her cousin instead. Skelmersdale tries desperately to come to terms with his experience, haunting the Knoll by night and calling hope-lessly to his lost lover. Sadly, she has gone forever, and Fairyland is closed to him. Ridiculed by his fellows, he leaves his village and moves to Bignor. However, when his secret emerges, he is jeered once more and the story ends with him consumed by unappeasable longing. 'There was something in his eyes and manner that was too difficult for him to express in words,' the narrator concludes (898), and Skelmersdale leaves with a 'wan smile', the mystery of what happened to him unresolved. 'Whether it really happened, whether he imagined or dreamt it, or fell upon it in some strange hallucinatory trance, I do not profess to say,' observes the narrator, 'But that he invented it I will not for one moment entertain' (888).

Wells's story uses a number of traditional fairy motifs, interweaving them with elements of Victorian and Romantic fairy lore, just as it mixes contemporary language with archaic vocabulary and word order in the description of Skelmersdale's flight from the gnomes. The *London Magazine*'s great rival, *The Strand*, had printed fairy stories in imitation of Andrew Lang's coloured 'fairy books' since the early 1890s, collecting them in a series of anthologies between 1894 and 1900 (Ashley 332), as well as publishing a number of Wells's short stories. Wells could therefore count on his readers (perhaps 'fans' would be a better word) being familiar with generic conventions and capable of appreciating his play with them. In this story, access to Fairyland is gained through a fairy ring on a fairy mound, a place that brings an unspecified doom upon those who meddle with it. 'There's a-many have tried to dig on Aldington Knoll,' says a village elder, 'But there's none as goes about to-day to tell what they got by digging' (887). The fairy world is protected by a barrier of thorns and briars, akin to the impenetrable foliage surrounding Sleeping Beauty in Charles Perrault's *La belle au bois dormant* (1696). Skelmersdale's uncertainty about the date of his experience may mean it occurred on Midsummer's Eve, 'one of the key nights for love divination' (Simpson & Roud 239) and a favourite date for stories of impossible romances between humans and supernatural beings. In Fairyland, Skelmersdale finds himself '*small*' and surrounded by 'a number of people still smaller', though this is neither surprising nor frightening to him (Wells 890). He is a 'comely youth' (891) who, like Tam Lin and others before him, catches the eye of the fairies as a result of his beauty. This makes him a suitable consort for the Fairy Lady, since she is of surpassing loveliness, dressed in 'filmy green' with 'a broad silver girdle' and 'a little tiara set with a silver star' (891). She is also prepared to grant her human love his 'heart's desire' (892) though, as usual in such tales, the wish does not work out exactly as he might have hoped. Fairy love and fairy gold cannot be brought back to Earth, and Skelmersdale is left with neither.

As in other fairy narratives, time passes at a different rate in Fairyland, and Skelmersdale is fortunate that only three weeks elapse while he is away. Finally, the experience of being in Fairyland, and the disbelief and ridicule that his story engenders, leaves him a melancholy shadow of his former self, like the Cornish farmer Mr Noy in Bottrell's *Traditions and Hearthside Stories of West Cornwall* (1870-80), a man who, as Katharine Briggs notes, 'Like many other visitors to Fairyland [. . .] pined and lost all interest in life after [his] adventure' (Briggs 158). Whatever happened to Skelmersdale defies linguistic representation, though the more educated narrator attributes his failure to describe the fairies as the result of a 'vague and imperfect' vocabulary and an 'unobservant' eye for detail (Wells 890).

Wells uses ingredients from fairy painting as well as from folklore, with Skelmersdale reporting that the fairies rode around on 'things' which the narrator surmises to have been 'Larvae, perhaps, or crickets, or the little beetles that elude us so abundantly' (891). The fairy tableaux he describes seem markedly reminiscent of pictures by notable Victorian painters such as John Anster Fitzgerald, Richard Dadd and Joseph Noel Paton:

> There was a place where water splashed and gigantic king-cups grew, and there in the hotter times the fairies bathed together. There were games being played and dancing and much elvish love making, too, I think, among the moss branch thickets. (892)

At last the Fairy Lady 'talked to [Skelmersdale] of love' in surroundings that recall the 'elfin grot' of Keats's 'La Belle Dame Sans Merci' (1819): unlike the hapless Knight-at-Arms, Wells's protagonist is spared nightmare, though he is left equally 'haggard' and 'woe-begone' (Keats 613). Skelmersdale is drawn to the Lady's beautiful neck, a frequent area of erotic attraction in the painting of the Pre-Raphaelites and their followers, but notes too the 'soft lines of a little child in her chin and cheeks and throat' (890). This may suggest that he, or the narrator, is reconfiguring his observations in line with the prevailing fairy imagery of the period, or, more sinisterly, the undercurrent of quasi-paedophilic desire found in 1890s' writers such as Ernest Dowson or certain fans of child music hall performers, most famously Cissie Loftus. The story is thus a mixture of ancient and modern elements, displaying the 'constant interplay between oral and printed transmission' (Westwood & Simpson vii) often noted as characteristic of folklore's development. One could even suggest that the narrator's retelling of Skelmersdale's experience makes him analogous to the collectors of folklore and song who tried to record what they believed to be the last remnants of a pre-industrial English culture in the early twentieth century. The members of the Folk-Lore Society, founded in 1878, and the Folk Song Society, founded twenty years later, were often guilty of sanitising the material they collected for middle class ears. Wells was not directly involved in either organisation, but he knew figures such as Edward Clodd, the president of the Folk-Lore Society from 1896 onwards, and may even have seen collectors in action in Kent and Sussex during the early 1900s.

Using Fairy Tales

In essence, there are two main reasons for Wells's use of the fairy story. The first is given by J.R. Hammond, who observes that 'Mr Skelmersdale' is 'notable for its preoccupation with a theme which was to haunt [Wells's] writings as a *leitmotiv* throughout his life'. This is 'that of a man who is obsessed by a vision of a beautiful, elusive lady and who searches in vain for the promise the vision seems to embody' (Hammond 68). Wells had recently explored this theme in his novel *The Sea Lady* (1902), and would return to it in the short story 'The Door in the Wall' (1906). Here Fairyland is reworked as an enchanted garden from the pictures of Waterhouse or Burne-Jones, complete with tame panthers and a 'sombre, dark woman with a grave, pale face and dreamy eyes' who wears 'a soft long robe of pale purple' (Wells, *Door* 150). The lost beloved reappears in more realistic surroundings in the condition-of-England novels *Tono-Bungay* (1909) and *The New Machiavelli* (1911), and surfaced in *Apropos of Dolores* as late as 1938. Nonetheless, 'Mr Skelmersdale' is the only time in which Wells enacts this story through explicit reference to the fairy tale, which leads to the second reason for his writing it.

'Mr Skelmersdale' is a rebuke to the increasingly senti-mental fairies of mainstream Victoriana, a tradition that was to reach its apotheosis in J.M. Barrie's *Peter Pan* (1904). Instead, Wells looks at the concerns of older types of fairy story through twentieth century eyes, offering not the moral teaching of children's fiction but rather a mixture of folklore, romanticism and the incomplete closure of modern narrative that provides a fresh perspective on fairy storytelling. With its unproven and inexplicable events, anecdotal style, dual narration and downbeat ending, 'Mr Skelmersdale' is moving in similar territory to fiction such as Rudyard Kipling's equally tall tale, 'The Man who would be King' (1888), a story that concludes 'And there the matter rests' (Kipling 140), without attempting to tie up its loose ends. The relaying of an incredible experience from a storyteller to a more formally educated narrator is also the technique used by Wells's friend Joseph Conrad in *Heart of Darkness*

(1899/1902). Wells's story seems almost artless in such exalted company, yet his use of similarly mediating narrative strategies suggests that it is more ambitious than it at first appears. Nothing in 'Mr Skelmersdale' is independently verifiable or inarguable, with Wells connecting sophisticated contemporary narrative modes and indeed, the psychiatric case study, with the more established conventions of oral tradition. It is this dynamic fusion of styles that leads one to argue that 'Mr Skelmersdale' is an example of that much-abused genre, the fairy tale for adults. The genre becomes a means by which Wells can explore his favourite theme of the lost woman and rescue the fairy story from the hands of Victorian sentimentalists while also carrying out furtively ambitious experiments in narrative technique.

Of course, he was not alone in taking the late Victorian fairy story out of the nursery, for during the 1890s it became imbued with political significance in the work of Irish writers such as W.B. Yeats, Augusta Gregory and George Russell ('A.E.'). Wells had also seen fairies assume a dark and frightening guise in Arthur Machen's 'The Shining Pyramid' and *The Three Impostors* (both 1895), where the 'fairies' of the Welsh hills are in fact a malign ancient race that preys upon unwary humans. Clearly, the fairy story did not have to surrender to the 'paroxysms of soppy joy' (Purkiss 256) that so appalled Diane Purkiss. Wells took a different tack from the Celtic writers, locating his fairies in rural South-Eastern England, the same region enchanted by Kipling's *Puck of Pook's Hill* (1906). He also cross-fertilised the fairy tale with the study of archaeology, anthropology and folklore that had begun to reimagine Kent and Sussex in the late Victorian period (Purkiss 263). Aldington Knoll is both a fairy hill and a prehistoric barrow, the type of structure that had inter-ested Andrew Lang, Grant Allen and J.G. Frazer (Parrinder 171-174), and the narrator suggests it be excavated. However, despite their differences of approach, each of these writers, Yeats, Machen, and Wells, wanted the fairy story to serve serious purposes rather than remaining a quaint relic of a more purportedly 'innocent' age.

What are these purposes? Perhaps the most important is a critique of human pettiness. The people who mock Skelmersdale are, unfortunately, typical of the majority of the late Victorian public, individuals attuned to the pursuit of material profit rather than the reverence of the imagination. This Dickensian opposition of fancy and practicality is also explored in 'The Door in the Wall', which pointedly tells of an imaginative child whose claims to have visited an enchanted garden win him first a thrashing at the hands of a resolutely dour Victorian *paterfamilias* and then the confiscation of his 'fairy-tale books' on the grounds that he is 'too "imaginative"' (Wells, *Door* 152). The earlier story ranges Skelmersdale's partially understood visionary experiences against 'the usual village shop, post-office, telegraph wire on its brow, zinc pans and brushes outside, boots, shirtings, and potted meats in the window' (Wells 884). It also places Skelsmersdale, imaginative but uneducated, a sort of peasant savant, against the forces of modern rationality. These take the forms of the narrator's pretentious 'spiritual pathology', which continually seeks to recast Skelmersdale's experience in more 'learned' and articulate language, and the medical science of the village doctor who dismisses Fairyland, preferring to talk about 'modern sanitary methods' (884) instead.

A decade later, Wells's Alfred Polly would revisit Skelmersdale's world, abandoned by a beautiful girl who is his social superior (Wells, *Polly* 64-71) and forced to work as a shopkeeper in a stifling country town. Polly is able to escape from dreary daily responsibility and begin his life anew at a country inn, but Skelmersdale is trapped in Bignor.

What makes his plight all the more dreadful is that it is in part a consequence of his internalising the dominant ideologies of the day. Without his longing for respectability expressed in the form of a little shop and marriage to a local girl, he could have remained with the Fairy Lady forever in willing rather than imposed servitude. Economic and social pressures have combined to rob Skelmersdale of eternal bliss, doing what Christian guilt had done to Tannhauser in medieval legend. The socialist bohemian author who was to join the Fabian Society in 1903 archly counterpoints the fairy world with the attritional banality of life in a country village to highlight what he called elsewhere 'the sort of gravitational pull back to the discipline and obedience of home' (Wells, *Door* 148). The antiquity of the fairy story genre allows Wells to juxtapose modern England, a place of zinc pans, 'spiritual pathology' and 'Married and Single' cricket matches (884), with the enduring world of the imagination, the world within that the Knoll may be said to symbolise.

The fairy story also allows sexual and social transgression, legitimating relationships across class boundaries. This may have made it particularly appealing to a political radical working within a rigidly hierarchical society, but because it employs a fantasy setting, it is still able to side-step the 'real world' overtones of this social organisation. This in turn allows Wells to indulge in the stereotypical objectificaton of the Fairy Lady: after all, neither of his storytellers is as politically radical as he is himself, and the *London Magazine* was essentially conservative in outlook. The woman remains unalterably 'other' by virtue of her fairy origins, but she is also far removed from Skelmersdale in terms of her gender and clearly fascinates the narrator whose own emotional life is noticeably barren. Is Wells accepting prevailing orthodoxy in suggesting that aristocratic women must remain *terra incognita* to working class men (and vice versa)? Does he imply that any such union will be based purely on physical attraction and is thus destined to be both transient and unhappy? Is he instead using the fairy tale to air questions that it would be inappropriate to pursue, let alone resolve, in the pages of a family magazine?

I am not of course suggesting that 'Mr Skelmersdale' represents a magical precursor of Lawrence's *Lady Chatterley's Lover* (1930), only that it demonstrates a tension in Wells's political thinking. He seems to oscillate between the stability afforded by marriage, stability which sometimes came at the price of self-denial, and the riskier 'free unions' governed by mutual affection that were debated by contemporary sexual radicals and memorably attempted in Thomas Hardy's *Jude the Obscure* (1895). Wells was invariably impatient with marital convention, abandoning his first wife for one of his students, and then, married once more, continuing to pursue extra-marital affairs while criticising conventional marriage in his work. With Skelmersdale forever exiled from Fairyland, however, issues of fidelity and union do not need to be resolved: Wells is able to hide his views, however inconsistent they may be, behind a smoke-screen of generic tradition that decrees the impossibility of love between humans and fairies. Also, since the Fairy Lady remains firmly in Fairyland, her opinions on the matter can go safely unrecorded.

'Mr Skelmersdale' allows Wells to rebuke certain elements of contemporary society, particularly the small-minded provincialism and material greed he despised throughout his life. However, it also allowed him to review some of his attitudes without necessarily seeming inconsistent: we have already seen how useful a Fairy Lady could be in contemplating women and sex from a safe distance. Equally surprising is the story's treatment of science and education, two topics Wells frequently championed in the early twentieth century. I suspect that by bringing these into contact with the numinous or magical, he is offering a cautionary check to positivist enthusiasm for the two as universal panaceas, and warning humanity about the perils of explaining and documenting every aspect of life. This he had done to some extent in his romances, with Dr. Moreau an especially powerful indictment of the folly of placing the search for knowledge before humanitarian concerns. 'Mr Skelmersdale' however gives a new twist to this technique, turning its attention to legend and myth rather than questions of physiology. The old man's rebuttal of the suggestion that the Knoll be excavated surely goes against the movement in British archaeology that would culminate in the great Sutton Hoo dig of 1939, a movement that Wells's contemporary, M.R. James, would also warn against in his chilling story 'A Warning to the Curious' (1925).

Additionally, it confronts Wells's readers with a stark question. What would they prefer, an excavated and catalogued Neolithic burial chamber, or the legends of fairies under the hill? From a reading of Wells's non-fiction, one would generally assume the former, but perhaps even he was suspicious of the desire to account for every aspect of life. After all, as a novelist who made his living and reputation from imaginative invention rather than didactic social commentary, he would have been reckless to promote its alternatives too enthusiastically. Likewise, the recasting of Skelmersdale's heart-felt story into altogether more 'educated' style robs it of much of its impact. Tellingly, it is only when the narrator submits to a poetic impulse and derives his imagery from the very world that Skelmersdale saw, that it revives. The Fairy Lady, spot-lit by the narrator's erotic fascination with her, 'shone clear amidst the muddle of his story like a glow-worm in a tangle of weeds' (894).

Conclusion

'Mr Skelmersdale in Fairyland' is one of the slighter stories in the Wells canon, but it is important for several reasons. As Hammond notes, it is another example of a crucial *leitmotiv* in Wells's writing. It also shows Wells struggling to overcome his Victorian inheritance by joining the ranks of those who sought to imbue a declining, increasingly juvenile form with fresh vigour. It raises sexual and social questions about early twentieth century England and taps into a number of contemporary preoccupations while yet remaining an engaging pastiche of a traditional story. It was Wells's ability to be radical and experimental while yet embedding these qualities in highly readable narratives of a seemingly familiar type that made him such a formidable presence in Edwardian literature. At the same time, the story showed that the fairy tale did not need to be extravagantly reworked in order to strike a chord with its readers. Skelmersdale's inability to express the wonder he has experienced, and the air of melancholy that hangs over his departure gives his tale a haunting quality that it retains a hundred years after its original publication.

Dr. Nick Freeman teaches English at the University of the West of England. He has published widely on 19th and 20th century literature, and has a particular interest in fantasy and paganism in late Victorian writing.

Works Cited

Ashley, Mike. 'Fairytale'. *The Encyclopedia of Fantasy*. Ed. John Clute and John Grant. London: Orbit, 1997.

Briggs, Katharine M. *British Folk-Tales and Legends: A Sampler.* London: Paladin, 1977.

Conrad, Joseph. *Heart of Darkness: A Simple Tale* in *Youth: A Narrative and Two Other Stories.* London: Blackwood, 1902.

Hammond, J.R. *An H.G. Wells Companion.* London & Basingstoke: Macmillan, 1979.

Keats, John. 'La Belle Dame Sans Merci'. *The New Oxford Book of English Verse 1250-1950.* Ed. Helen Gardner. Oxford: Oxford University Press, 1972: 613-14.

Kipling, Rudyard. *The Man who would be King* [1888]. Kipling, *Selected Stories.* Ed. Andrew Rutherford. London: Penguin, 1987.

Lester Jr., John A. *Journey Through Despair 1880-1914: Transformations in British Literary Culture.* Princeton: Princeton University Press, 1968.

Machen, Arthur. *The Three Impostors or The Transmutations.* London: John Lane, 1895.

_____. 'The Shining Pyramid' [1895]. Machen, *Tales of Horror and the Supernatural.* London: Panther, 1963: 7-30.

Parrinder, Patrick. 'The Old Man and His Ghost: Grant Allen, H.G. Wells, and Popular Anthropology' in *Grant Allen: Literature and Cultural Politics at the Fin de Siècle.* Ed. William Greenslade & Terence Rogers. Aldershot: Ashgate, 2005, 171-83.

Purkiss, Diane. *At the Bottom of the Garden: A Dark History of Fairies, Hobgoblins, and Other Troublesome Things.* New York: New York University Press, 2000.

Simpson, Jacqueline, & Steve Roud. *A Dictionary of English Folklore.* Oxford: Oxford University Press, 2000.

Wells, H.G. 'Mr. Skelsmerdale in Fairyland' [1901]. *The Complete Short Stories of H.G. Wells.* London: Ernest Benn, 1927: 884-98.

_____. 'The Door in the Wall' [1906]. *The Complete Stories of H.G. Wells:* 144-161.

_____. *The History of Mr Polly* [1910]. Ed. Norman Mackenzie. London: Dent, 1993.

Westwood, Jennifer, & Jacqueline Simpson. *The Lore of the Land.* London: Penguin, 2005.

Wood, Christopher. *Fairies in Victorian Art.* Woodbridge: Antique Collectors' Club, 2000.

About the Editrices

Helen Pilinovsky (Articles Editor) is a folklore scholar who is currently pursuing doctoral studies at Columbia University in the department of English and Comparative Literature. She has had articles published at the Endicott Studio website and in *Realms of Fantasy* magazine, and has had reviews placed in *Marvels & Tales: The Journal of Fairy Tale Studies*, and in the *New York Review of Science Fiction*. She has guest edited issues of Extrapolation and The Journal of the Fantastic in the Arts, and is now completing her dissertation on the translation and acculturation of the fairy tale.

Catherynne M. Valente (Advisor) is a poet, author and scholar whose work can be found online and in print in such journals as *Pedestal Magazine*, *Fantastic Metropolis*, *Jabberwocky*, *Fantasy Magazine* and is featured in *The Year's Best Fantasy and Horror #18*. Her critical series on feminine archetypes in Greek and Roman drama has appeared in successive issues of the *International Journal of the Humanities*. Her latest novel, *Yume no Hon: The Book of Dreams*, was recently published by Prime Books. Her four-book series of interconnected fairy tales in the tradition of *Arabian Nights*, *The Orphan's Tales*, will be released by Bantam/Dell in fall 2007. Her website has more information about her projects: http://www.catherynnemvalente.com/

Erzebet Barthold-YellowBoy (Fiction Editor) is a writer, bookbinder and artist. Her short stories have appeared in *Elysian Fiction* and *Fantasy Magazine* and are forthcoming in *Jabberwocky 2* and other places. In 2001 she founded Papaveria Press, a private press specializing in fairy tales and fantastic visions. When she is not writing or binding books, she plays with bones. Using natural elements to reshape and revisit myth and folktales, each of her bone panels includes a small poem or microtale on the back. A sampling of her work can be seen at http://www.erzebet.com.

Printed in the United States
53323LVS00001B/40